# SATELLITES
# & SPACE STATIONS

## Moira Butterfield

Designed by **Iain Ashman**

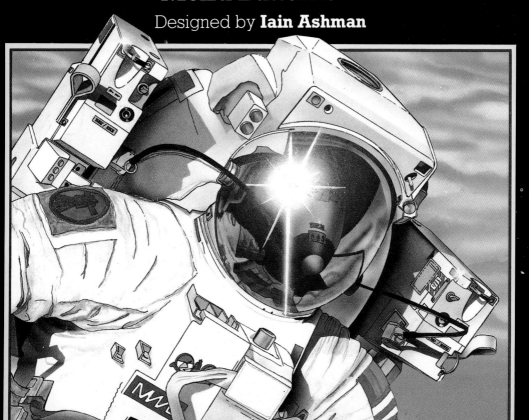

Consultant Editor: **Sue Becklake**

Editor: **Tony Potter**

Orbit program: **Chris Oxlade**

Consultants: **Geoffrey Pardoe, Robin Kerrod, John Hawkins.**

Illustrated by: **Peter Bull, Chris Lyon, Guy Smith, Richard Draper, Stuart Trotter, Roger Stewart, Martin Newton, Jeremy Gower.**

Additional designs: **Winsome Malcolm, Barbara Wightman,**

# CONTENTS

# About satellites and space stations

A modern communications satellite

← Sputnik 1

This book explains what satellites and space stations are, what they do and how they work. A satellite is an object in space which goes around (orbits) a larger object, such as a planet. There are natural satellites, such as the Moon, but this book is concerned with artificial ones.

The first artificial satellite, Sputnik 1, was launched by Russia in 1957. It was a sphere, the size of a large beachball, and it worked for 23 days. Satellites today are much more complicated. They can be the size of a two-storey house, with working lifetimes of up to ten years. There are over 5,000 of many different kinds in orbit.

Space stations are satellites too, because they orbit Earth. But they are manned, and have special features

Astronauts are weightless in a space station.

such as living quarters and science laboratories. Space station astronauts carry out scientific experiments, take photos of Earth and space, and sometimes launch or repair other satellites. You can find out about their work in this book, and what it is like to live in a space station.

Unmanned satellites do many vital jobs. The most useful kind are communications satellites, which relay telephone calls, TV programs and

other information between different locations on Earth. Soon it will become possible for everyone to receive these satellite signals directly into their own homes, using small receiving dishes.

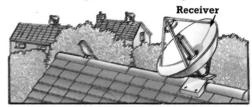

Receiver

Satellites and space stations also carry special equipment to survey areas of Earth and space. They get a good view of Earth because they orbit high above it, and a good view of space because they are above the Earth's murky atmosphere.

Satellite technology is developing rapidly. This book shows some of the exciting future projects planned, when satellites will link the whole world, and people will start making permanent homes in space.

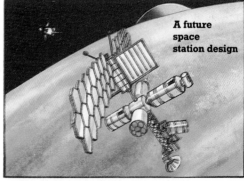

A future space station design

At the back of the book there is a computer program for putting imaginary satellites into orbit. You can use it with Commodore 64, MSX, BBC, VIC-20, Spectrum, Apple, Electron, and TRS-80 computers.

# How satellites work

Unmanned satellites do various sorts of jobs and they look very different from each other. But they all carry certain items of basic equipment for power, control and protection, for instance. All satellites have an antenna (or aerial) attached called a command antenna, which relays "house-keeping" signals to Earth about the satellite's internal workings and its position in orbit. There is also special equipment on board for the satellite's own particular job. Communications satellites, for example, have special communications antennas, which relay signals such as TV or telephone messages, between two ground receiving dishes on Earth.

## Comstar 1

The communications satellite Comstar 1 is shown in the cutaway picture on the right. It carries typical satellite equipment, labelled in the yellow boxes. It is 5.2m (17ft) high, 2.3m (7.5ft) wide, and weighs about the same as 18 average sized men. You can find out more about some of the parts on later pages, as shown in each box.

## What satellites do

The pictures below represent the different kinds of jobs satellites do. You can find out more about each of them later in this book.

Communications satellites receive signals such as telephone calls from Earth. They relay the signals to a different place on Earth.

Navigation satellite signals help sailors and pilots pin-point their own position. Satellites also relay ship-to-shore communications.

Earth resources satellites collect measurements of radiation from land and sea. This data is converted into images for scientific study.

Weather satellites gather temperature and other information about land, sea and clouds. This is converted into measurements and images of the weather.

Military satellites spy on weapons, armies and secret bases. They also relay coded signals between soldiers. Some can destroy enemy satellites.

Scientific satellites pin-point and measure radiation sources coming from space, helping scientists discover new objects in the universe.

# Comstar parts

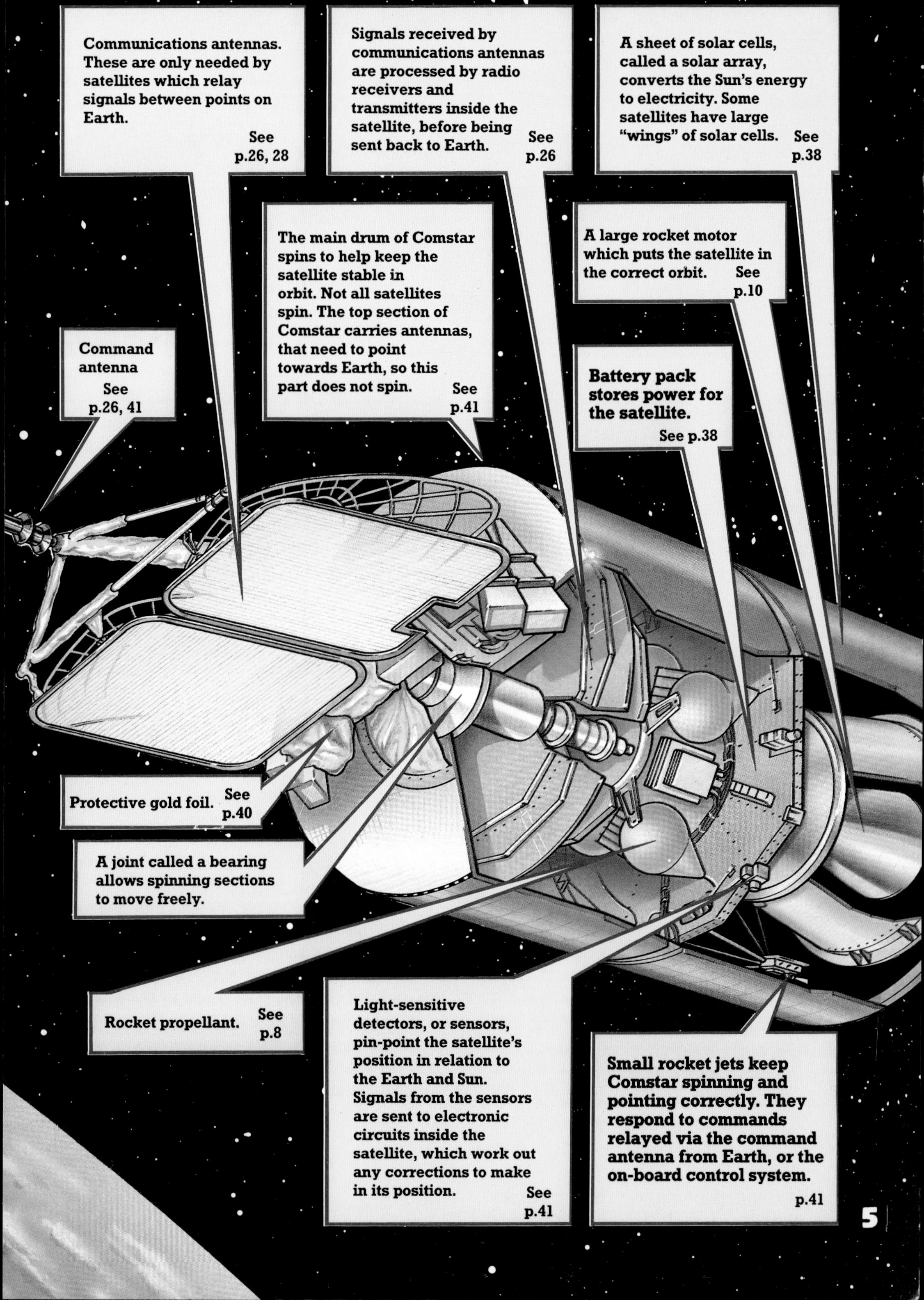

Communications antennas. These are only needed by satellites which relay signals between points on Earth.
See p.26, 28

Signals received by communications antennas are processed by radio receivers and transmitters inside the satellite, before being sent back to Earth.
See p.26

A sheet of solar cells, called a solar array, converts the Sun's energy to electricity. Some satellites have large "wings" of solar cells.
See p.38

The main drum of Comstar spins to help keep the satellite stable in orbit. Not all satellites spin. The top section of Comstar carries antennas, that need to point towards Earth, so this part does not spin.
See p.41

A large rocket motor which puts the satellite in the correct orbit.
See p.10

Command antenna
See p.26, 41

Battery pack stores power for the satellite.
See p.38

Protective gold foil.
See p.40

A joint called a bearing allows spinning sections to move freely.

Rocket propellant.
See p.8

Light-sensitive detectors, or sensors, pin-point the satellite's position in relation to the Earth and Sun. Signals from the sensors are sent to electronic circuits inside the satellite, which work out any corrections to make in its position.
See p.41

Small rocket jets keep Comstar spinning and pointing correctly. They respond to commands relayed via the command antenna from Earth, or the on-board control system.
p.41

5

# Spacecraft and gravity

Gravity is the force that holds things to the surface of planets. Satellites are taken into space by rockets, which must travel upwards at a very high speed to counteract gravity. The satellites are then released into orbit. Once released, a satellite is held in orbit round the Earth by the effect of gravity. You can find out why this happens on these pages.

## What is gravity?

Gravity is a pulling force between objects. At least one of the objects has to be huge for the effect to be noticeable. Objects don't fall off the Earth because its gravitational effect is so large. The Earth's gravity keeps the Moon in orbit, but the Moon's effect on the Earth is smaller – only enough to cause the sea tides. The Sun has a huge gravitational pull, keeping Earth and the other planets in orbit around it. The effect of gravitational pull between two objects decreases the further apart they get.

**Strong pull of Earth on objects.**

**Strong pull of Earth on Moon.**  **Weak pull of Moon.**

## Mass and weight

The strength of an object's gravitational pull depends on the amount of material in it, called its mass. The Earth has an enormous mass, and a strong pull.

Weight is the measurement of a planet's pull on an object's mass. An object's mass remains the same on different planets, but its weight changes according to the planet's pull (which in turn depends on the planet's mass). In space, far from planets, there is only a tiny pull, called microgravity, which gives objects a minute weight.

## Gravity's pull

**Earth's pull**

**Ball pulled down.**

If you throw a ball vertically upwards, Earth's gravity exerts a downward pull on it as it travels up. This slows the ball down until it begins to fall back.

**Moon's weak pull.**

**Ball goes up a long way.**

The same ball thrown on the Moon would go much higher before falling to the ground. The Moon's mass is smaller than the Earth's, so the gravitational attraction between the ball and the Moon is weaker. This means it would take longer for the ball to slow down.

## A space orbit

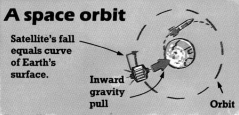

**Satellite's fall equals curve of Earth's surface.**

**Inward gravity pull**

**Orbit**

A satellite needs to be carried up by rocket at a very high speed to avoid being pulled back in the same way as the ball shown above. To go into orbit, the satellite has to be pushed sideways from the rocket at a speed dependent on its height from Earth. A satellite moving in a circle around the Earth falls towards the centre of the Earth due to gravity pull. But, because the Earth is round, its surface curves away, too.

If the satellite is going fast enough for its height, the amount it falls in a given time is equal to the curve of the Earth's surface, as though it were spinning round on a string attached to the Earth's centre. The satellite stays in orbit. This speed is called orbital velocity.

# Speed and gravity

The way that satellites stay in orbit is illustrated by the man below, who is whirling a bucket of water around like a windmill.

**1**

The water falls out of the bucket.

Pull of Earth's gravity.

First he whirls the bucket round slowly. The speed of the bucket and water sideways is small, and the force of gravity pulls the water nearer the Earth, so the man gets wet.

**2**

The water stays in the bucket.

As he whirls the bucket round faster the water goes at the right speed to stay in the bucket, in the same way that satellites go at the right speed to stay in orbit.

**3**

The bucket and water pull away from the man.

If the bucket of water is whirled round even faster it begins to pull away from the man. If a satellite goes faster than its original velocity it moves outwards into a different orbit.

The nearer a satellite's orbit is to Earth, the stronger the gravity pull on it. The satellite must go faster to remain in the smaller orbit.

## Weightlessness

Inside a spaceship orbiting Earth astronauts float and cannot stand still on the floor unless they hold onto something. An astronaut and all the unsecured contents of the ship act in relation to the floor in the same way that the spacecraft acts in relation to the Earth. They keep falling, due to gravitational pull, but the floor is falling too, and they can never catch up with it. They float, apparently weightlessly.

## Space sailors

The word "astronaut" derives from Greek and Latin, and means star sailor.
Russian spacemen are called cosmonauts, which means sailors of the cosmos.

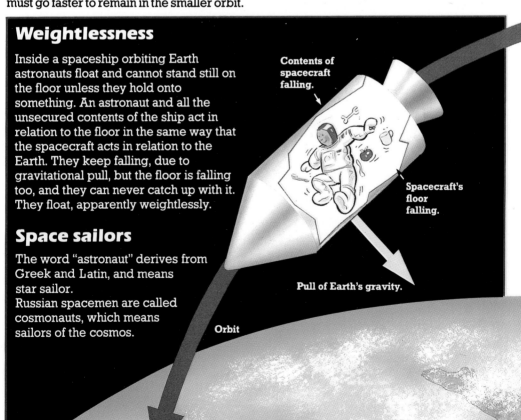

Contents of spacecraft falling.

Spacecraft's floor falling.

Pull of Earth's gravity.

Orbit

# Escape from Earth

Satellites must be taken up into space and released at the right speed to stay in orbit. They are released from the nosecones of unmanned rockets or from the cargo bay of the Space Shuttle, once it is in orbit. All rockets work on the principle that an action in one direction causes an equal reaction in the opposite direction. You can see how this works if you let go of a blown-up balloon. The air rushes out one way, making the balloon move the other way. This effect is caused in rockets by burning liquid or solid fuel.

## How a liquid fuel rocket works

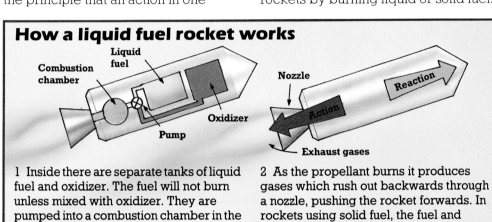

1 Inside there are separate tanks of liquid fuel and oxidizer. The fuel will not burn unless mixed with oxidizer. They are pumped into a combustion chamber in the engine, where a spark sets them alight. They are called a propellant when mixed.

2 As the propellant burns it produces gases which rush out backwards through a nozzle, pushing the rocket forwards. In rockets using solid fuel, the fuel and oxidizer are not in separate tanks. They are already mixed together in a rubbery material.

## Rocket stages

This is Ariane, an unmanned launch rocket. To develop enough power to escape gravity it has three parts on top of each other, called stages, each with its own fuel supply and engine nozzle. One by one each stage uses up its fuel supply and drops away. The top stage releases a satellite into an orbit called a transfer orbit (see page 10).

**3rd stage**

**2nd stage**

**1st stage**

1st stage oxidizer tank

1st stage fuel tank

Ariane was developed by the European Space Agency, ESA for short.

## Ariane launch pattern

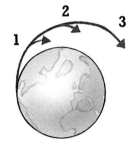

1st stage separates at height of 43km (27 miles).

2nd stage separates at height of 300km (186 miles).

3rd stage sends satellite into orbit. Stages burn up.

## The Space Shuttle launch

The Space Shuttle differs from conventional rockets, like Ariane, because most of it can be reused. It is launched into orbit, just like a rocket, but carrying crew as well as satellites. The Orbiter has three rocket engines fuelled by a huge external tank. It also has two solid-fuel rocket boosters (shown on the right) to give it enough power to reach orbit.

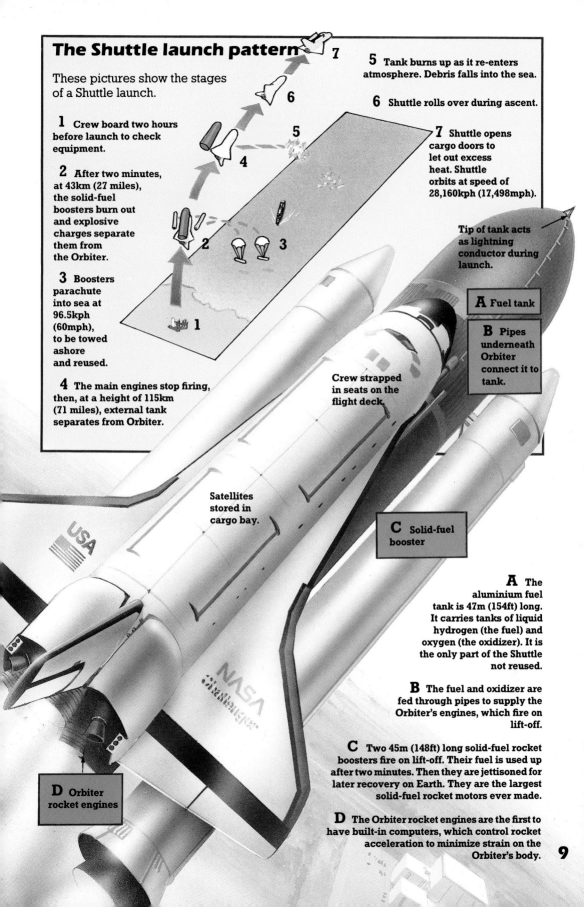

# The Shuttle launch pattern

These pictures show the stages of a Shuttle launch.

**1** Crew board two hours before launch to check equipment.

**2** After two minutes, at 43km (27 miles), the solid-fuel boosters burn out and explosive charges separate them from the Orbiter.

**3** Boosters parachute into sea at 96.5kph (60mph), to be towed ashore and reused.

**4** The main engines stop firing, then, at a height of 115km (71 miles), external tank separates from Orbiter.

**5** Tank burns up as it re-enters atmosphere. Debris falls into the sea.

**6** Shuttle rolls over during ascent.

**7** Shuttle opens cargo doors to let out excess heat. Shuttle orbits at speed of 28,160kph (17,498mph).

Tip of tank acts as lightning conductor during launch.

**A** Fuel tank

**B** Pipes underneath Orbiter connect it to tank.

Crew strapped in seats on the flight deck.

Satellites stored in cargo bay.

**C** Solid-fuel booster

**A** The aluminium fuel tank is 47m (154ft) long. It carries tanks of liquid hydrogen (the fuel) and oxygen (the oxidizer). It is the only part of the Shuttle not reused.

**B** The fuel and oxidizer are fed through pipes to supply the Orbiter's engines, which fire on lift-off.

**C** Two 45m (148ft) long solid-fuel rocket boosters fire on lift-off. Their fuel is used up after two minutes. Then they are jettisoned for later recovery on Earth. They are the largest solid-fuel rocket motors ever made.

**D** Orbiter rocket engines

**D** The Orbiter rocket engines are the first to have built-in computers, which control rocket acceleration to minimize strain on the Orbiter's body.

**9**

# Orbit round the Earth

Satellites and space stations can orbit at almost any height above Earth's surface, providing they move at the correct speed to counteract the pull of gravity at that height. The orbit chosen depends on the job the spacecraft has to do. Satellites can orbit directly above the Equator, or pass over the Poles, or at any angle between the two.

## The shape of orbits

Satellite orbits trace out a shape called an ellipse. A circle is actually a special kind of ellipse, so orbits can also be circular. A very long narrow ellipse is called eccentric, as shown below. This orbit is used by satellites that swoop low to look at the Earth – spy satellites, for example. In an orbit that is not circular the speed of the satellite changes all the time. But in a circular orbit it remains the same.

An eccentric orbit

## Non-circular orbits

To go into a non-circular orbit a satellite is released from a rocket in an upward curve away from the Earth. As it travels up against the pull of gravity the satellite loses speed. The furthest point of its orbit is called the apogee. Here the satellite is moving at its lowest speed, and it begins to be pulled back downwards by gravity.

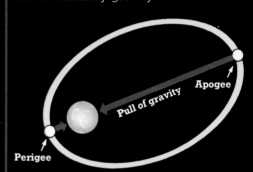

The lowest point of the satellite's orbit is called the perigee. Here it is moving at its maximum speed, and is fast enough to start moving away from Earth. The points of apogee and perigee in an orbit depend on the direction and speed of the satellite when released.

## Transfer orbits

Sometimes a satellite designed to go in a high circular orbit is first placed in a low orbit by a rocket or the Space Shuttle.

From here a small rocket engine on the satellite, called the perigee kick motor, fires to place the satellite in a non-circular "transfer" orbit, shown below.

At the furthest point of the orbit, a similar rocket engine, called an apogee kick motor, puts the satellite in high orbit.

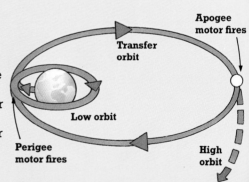

## Atmospheric drag

Air molecules in the atmosphere are kept around the Earth by the force of gravity. If a satellite passes through the atmosphere, it has to push against the air molecules and it slows down. Eventually it will no longer be going fast enough to counteract the pull of gravity. It will fall towards Earth and burn up in the atmosphere. Atmospheric drag is not noticeable above about 500km (311 miles).

# Different kinds of orbit

The picture on this page shows three important kinds of satellite orbit.

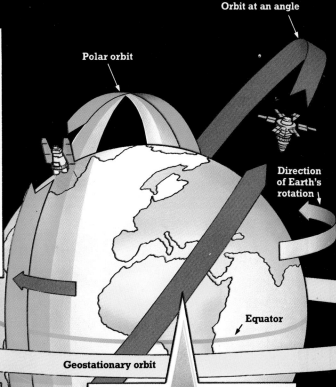

**Orbit at an angle**

**Polar orbit**

**Direction of Earth's rotation**

**Equator**

**Geostationary orbit**

## Geostationary

At a height of 35,786km (22,237 miles) a satellite takes 24 hours to circle Earth, the same time as the Earth takes to spin round its axis. A satellite in this orbit directly above the Equator, going eastward as the Earth does, stays above the same point on Earth. This is called geostationary orbit, and is used by many types of satellite. Ground tracking stations can "see" a geostationary satellite in the same place in the sky at all times.

## Polar

A satellite travelling over both Poles is in a polar orbit. Earth resources and some weather satellites do this. Their low orbits usually take them round the Earth about 14 times a day. Each time they "see" a different area, as the Earth turns more slowly beneath them. They cover almost the whole planet surface after a few days. You can find out more about the jobs polar orbiting satellites do on page 30, and about a special near-polar orbit called Sun-synchronous.

## Orbits at an angle

Some Soviet communications satellites, called Molniyas, are put into an eccentric orbit at an angle to the Equator, so they travel slowly over Russia for a large part of their orbit. Similar orbits are also used if a country's launch sites are far from the Equator. It is difficult and costly to put satellites into geostationary orbit from these launch sites.

If you have a computer or can borrow one use the program at the end of this book to plot different kinds of satellite orbit.

## A satellite period

The time a satellite takes to travel one revolution round Earth is called its period, and is measured by the time it takes to return to a fixed point above Earth. For example, a satellite at 1,700km (1,056 miles) has a period of about two hours. The lower a satellite, the shorter the period will be.

# How a space station works

A space station is a kind of satellite with a crew on board. The American Skylab and the Russian Salyut series are the only long-term space stations that have gone into orbit so far. They have been used to study the effects of living in space, to survey Earth and for scientific experiments.

The American Space Shuttle isn't a true space station. It is really a ferry craft between Earth and space, looking more like a plane than a spaceship. But it acts as a space station during its nine to ten-day missions, when the crew launch and repair satellites and do scientific experiments.

The longest time a space station has stayed in orbit so far is six years (Salyut 6), but future stations will orbit permanently. These pages show the equipment used by all stations, long-term or temporary.

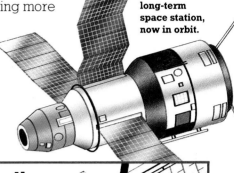

Salyut 7 – the latest long-term space station, now in orbit.

## 1 Computers

Shuttle computers

Computers operate the complex systems of a station, such as navigation and life support systems. The Shuttle's five computers have display consoles (shown above) on the flight deck. They are always in contact with computers on the ground.

## 2 Cooling

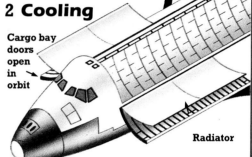

Cargo bay doors open in orbit

Radiator

Stations are cooled by liquid circulating through pipes. The liquid absorbs excess heat from station equipment. On the Shuttle it is piped via radiators inside the cargo bay doors, which are opened in orbit to lose heat into space.

## 3 Living and working sections

Mid-deck for living

Flight deck for working

Spacelab

Scientific equipment

Equipment deck

Space stations have small living areas, and working areas for station controls and scientific equipment. They also have storage areas for things like oxygen and water. The Shuttle nose is separated into three decks for these functions.

The Shuttle sometimes carries a laboratory called Spacelab in the cargo bay, together with open platforms for scientific equipment (see page 21). Salyut has outside scientific equipment attached to its shell.

# 4 Air

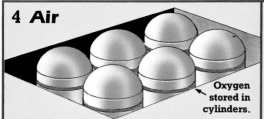

Oxygen stored in cylinders.

There must be air inside a station for the crew to breath, and to exert pressure on the outside of their bodies. If there were no pressure, the crews' blood would boil, and they would die. The air in a station is usually a mixture of oxygen and nitrogen gases, constantly filtered and recirculated. The control of air, water and temperature is called the life-support system.

# 5 Airlocks

Air     Vacuum

Inside door     Air in airlock     Vacuum     Outside door

If an ordinary door were opened from a station into space the air inside would be sucked out by the vacuum outside. So the crew use an airlock, a space between two airtight doors. They go through the first door and shut it tightly, as shown above. If they are wearing spacesuits they can let the air out to leave a vacuum, and then open the outer door. The airlock works the opposite way when they come in.

# 6 Protection

Strong double shell

Stations are built to withstand space debris. They have strong double-skinned aluminium shells to take the impact of any collision.

# 7 Payloads

Shuttle satellite launch

Payloads are items of cargo, such as scientific experiments, sometimes carried by space stations. They may be paid for by private companies. Satellites launched from the Shuttle cargo bay, as shown above, are payloads. Salyut stations only carry government payloads.

# 8 Power

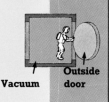

Skylab solar panel

Large space stations have huge solar cell panels to provide power. The Shuttle uses fuel cells instead, which combine oxygen and hydrogen to make electricity. Station manoeuvring engines use fuel stored on board.

# 9 Docking

Ferry craft from Earth have to dock with space stations. This means securely latching two spacecraft together. A docking port has pins which fit into holes on the incoming vehicle.

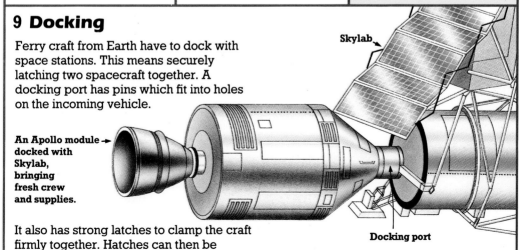

Skylab

An Apollo module docked with Skylab, bringing fresh crew and supplies.

Docking port

It also has strong latches to clamp the craft firmly together. Hatches can then be opened and people can move through.

**13**

# Living in space

Inside a space station everything floats due to the effect of gravity. Astronauts have had to find new ways of doing everyday things, like eating, sleeping and washing. All the tools and household items they use must be carefully secured, or they might cause damage by floating loose. They are held down magnetically, by clips, or a fastening of Velcro (trade name for a fastener made of two strips of fuzzy fabric).

**Unsecured objects float out if a space station cupboard is opened.**

## What it feels like

There is no up or down in space, but astronauts like to have all the equipment standing up the same way, so that it looks like there is a floor and a ceiling. Even so, many astronauts get space sickness (a sort of travel sickness), because their brain gets

confused when they float around. It usually takes about three days to get over space sickness, as the brain gets used to the body being weightless.

## Body changes

When a body is weightless its fluids tend to float upwards. An astronaut's face puffs up, his head feels stuffy, as though he has a cold, and his legs get thinner. People get a little taller too, as shown on the right, because the discs in the backbone are no longer squashed down by the pressure of gravity.

← Original Earth height

**14**

*See pages 6 and 7.

## An astronaut's day

The pictures on these pages show the most up-to-date living equipment used by crews during a day in a space station. Most of it is Shuttle equipment, developed from lessons learnt on board Skylab. Salyut cosmonauts live in much the same way, although their equipment is designed differently and, unlike the Shuttle crew, they live and work in one area. There is no regular day or night in space, but crews work to an artificial timetable. They sleep for about eight hours, and for the rest of the time work on things like experiments or repairs, with breaks for eating and relaxing.

## A space toilet

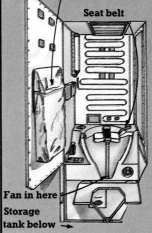

Rubbish bag

Seat belt

Fan in here

Storage tank below →

The picture on the left shows a Shuttle space toilet. Hand controls activate a fan which draws waste from the toilet down to storage tanks under the floor. Solids are automatically disinfected before storage.

## Eating

Space food is chosen to give a balanced, interesting diet. It is prepared to stay fresh for a long while, in cans, foil pouches and plastic containers. Foods like biscuits are stored in their "Earth" forms. Some food is dried (dehydrated) and water is added on board. More perishable food is cooked at low temperatures on Earth or treated with radiation to kill bacteria, before packing.

**Space food containers**

Pleats on Shuttle jacket.

Closed pockets

## Clothes

Astronauts wear comfortable clothes inside a station, like the ones above. Trousers have elasticated bottoms to stop them riding up, and lots of pockets which are fastened to stop objects floating out. Shuttle space jackets have elasticated pleats to stretch and fit an astronaut's new height. Before returning to Earth crews get used to gravity by wearing suits designed to pull body fluids back downwards.

## Keeping clean

Keeping clean and disposing of rubbish and body-wastes are especially important in the closed-in area of a space station. Rubbish is stored in tanks and later returned to Earth, sometimes on board docking craft. The picture above shows an enclosed Shuttle wash basin. It has two hand holes, water and soap dispensers. A fan at the back draws dirty water away to

a tank under the floor. When the tank is full an astronaut dumps the water overboard through an airlock.

Enclosed wash basin

## Staying put

Space station crew anchor themselves using handrails, footholds or suction cups, to stop weightlessness hampering them in their work. In weightless conditions feet tend to point downwards as though relaxed. This makes it hard to stand flat on the floor. On the Shuttle special boot attachments with anchoring suction cups have been developed to keep feet in a comfortable position, as shown on the right.

Heel support

Suction cups

## Exercise

Keep-fit equipment is essential on board, so the crew can exercise the muscles that normally hold them up against the pull of gravity on Earth, but are not used in space. There are usually treadmills and exercise bikes attached to a station floor. Sweat has to be vacuumed away by an air suction system next to exercise machines, because water does not drip off things in space.

Shuttle treadmill

Shoulder harness

Roller

Metal base

Food pantry

Oven

Meal trays

Water heater and storage

The picture on the left shows a Shuttle kitchen unit called a galley. It is a large dispensing machine with hot and cold water, cutlery, trays, a larder and a hot air oven. Food containers fit into the trays, which attach to a table magnetically.

Astronauts eat standing up, bringing food quickly up to their mouths. They do this to stop food floating off cutlery and hitting them.

Sleeping bag

Crewmember "upside down"

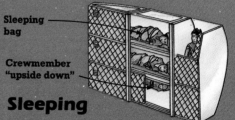

## Sleeping

The picture above shows how astronauts sleep in the Space Shuttle. On the mid-deck there is a "sleep station", with room for four people to sleep at once. Each bunk has a ventilated fireproof sleeping bag attached to a padded board. One member of the crew can sleep "upright", and one "upside down". This feels quite normal when weightless.

**15**

# Salyut and Skylab

These pages show the American Skylab and the Russian Salyut (a series of seven), the only space stations that have been sent into long-term orbit so far. Salyut 7 is still in orbit. Both types were launched to discover the effect on people of long periods in space, and to carry scientific experiments. They could be shut down when empty and automatically reactivated on crew arrival. Both types were built with space station essentials.

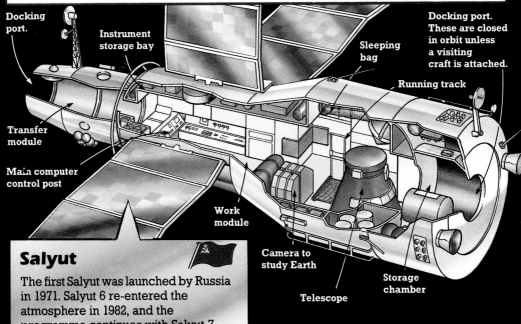

**Docking port.**

**Instrument storage bay**

**Transfer module**

**Main computer control post**

**Work module**

**Docking port.** These are closed in orbit unless a visiting craft is attached.

**Sleeping bag**

**Running track**

**Camera to study Earth**

**Telescope**

**Storage chamber**

## Salyut

The first Salyut was launched by Russia in 1971. Salyut 6 re-entered the atmosphere in 1982, and the programme continues with Salyut 7, launched in 1982. Salyut 7 is shown in the cutaway picture above. Each new station is modified as a result of discoveries on previous versions.

Salyut has a docking port at either end. Next to one of them is an airlock chamber called a transfer module, that connects the station to a visiting crewed ship. Robot craft called "Progress" vehicles, or manned Soyuz spacecraft, bring fresh supplies and crews to the station. Three craft were linked in space for the first time when craft docked to either end of Salyut 6.

Salyut is powered by solar cell arrays outside its main body, which is split into different sections, shown in the picture. They are used for living, working and storing equipment. The main section, called the work module, is used both for living and working. The long-term crews of Salyut 7 have set new records for time spent in space.

## Experiments in space

The Skylab and Salyut crews carried out many experiments in space. The main ones are listed below. You can find out more about making new products in space on page 20.

**A Salyut camera**

★ Cameras on both kinds of station took many photos of Earth. From these scientists were able to spot new landscape features, such as likely earthquake sites.

**Ordinary camera.**

★ Scientists monitored the crew reactions to living in space. All crews exercised regularly, while their heart rate, pulse and breathing was measured.

**On Salyut 7 an Indian cosmonaut tried yoga.**

# Major space repairs

During Skylab's launch a protective heat shield was torn off the main body, pulling off one of the large solar cell panels and jamming the other half-open. This left Skylab seriously underpowered and overheated. The picture on the right shows a protective sunshade which was erected over the workshop by the first Skylab crew. This brought the temperature down. They also managed to pull out the jammed panel. On Salyut 7 a large solar cell array was damaged and a broken pipe spilled fuel out into space. Extra solar panels were fitted, and the fuel system was repaired by spacewalking cosmonauts.

Sunshade

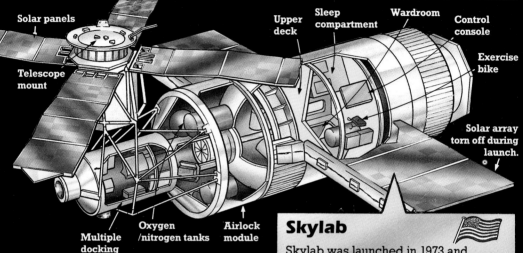

Solar panels

Telescope mount

Upper deck

Sleep compartment

Wardroom

Control console

Exercise bike

Solar array torn off during launch.

Multiple docking adaptor

Oxygen /nitrogen tanks

Airlock module

★ Skylab's telescopes studied activity on the Sun which could not be seen from Earth.

★ On both stations the crews made and tested new materials such as metals, glass and crystals. Salyut has two furnaces on board for manufacturing space products.

A Salyut furnace

★ Two spiders adapted to weightlessness in Skylab and spun normal webs. Minnows from Earth swam round in a tank on board, in tight circles at first, but those born in space swam normally.

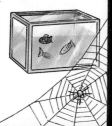

# Skylab

Skylab was launched in 1973 and burned up in the atmosphere in 1979, after carrying three separate crews. It was built from part of a Saturn V Moon rocket. The rocket's hydrogen tank was converted into the main section of Skylab, and the oxygen tank became a rubbish store. Added to the main section was a multiple docking adaptor, where Apollo Command Modules carrying crews from Earth could attach themselves. The crew moved between craft through an airlock module.

Above the docking adaptor was a platform called an Apollo telescope mount, carrying instruments to study the Sun. It had its own solar panels. Two other panels powered the main part of the station. One was damaged during launch, but the picture above shows them as they should have been.

The bottom deck of Skylab's main section had a wardroom (a lounge where the crew could relax and eat), sleeping compartments, a bathroom and experiments room.

# Building and repairing in space

The Space Shuttle is designed primarily as a ferry that will fly from Earth to future permanent space stations with astronauts and supplies. But its crew will also build space stations in space. The picture on the right shows how Shuttle astronauts might assemble such a station from sections built on Earth and taken up in Shuttle cargo bays. These pages show some of the equipment the crew will use on the "building site". Similar equipment will be used on the stations once in operation, to help future crews in their main work of repairing payloads, such as satellites.

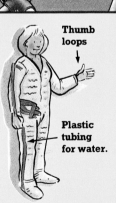

## The Shuttle crew

The Shuttle crew can be up to seven people. The crew of permanent stations will be larger, but their work will be similar to that of the Shuttle astronauts, shown below.

The Commander is in charge of the station. He decides what to do in an emergency.

The Pilot deputizes for the Commander and helps handle the vehicle's controls.

Mission Specialists are astronaut/scientists trained to deal with payload operations, such as repairing a satellite, and they help the Commander and Pilot with tasks such as navigation.

Payload Specialists are scientists, engineers or doctors who operate scientific payloads, such as Spacelab experiments.

## EVA

Shuttle astronauts go into space to repair equipment, or in the future to build new stations. This is called extra vehicular activity, or EVA for short. The crew wear pressurized spacesuits which supply them with oxygen. The steps on the right show how they put on a spacesuit.

**Thumb loops**

**Plastic tubing for water.**

**1** An undergarment goes on first. It has cooling water tubes and air ducts.

# Remote Manipulator System (RMS)

The RMS is a 15m (50ft) long jointed robot arm attached to the Shuttle cargo bay. It lifts satellites out for launch, or rescues them for repair. It will hold parts in position for astronauts building stations. It has its own computer programs, or can be operated manually. Cameras along the arm transmit pictures of its movements to the flight deck. A future station may have an RMS-type crane for launch and repair work. The RMS "hand", called an end effector, is used to grip a shaft (a "grapple fixture"), built on to Shuttle payloads.

End effector

Inside the end effector there are three wires. A ring attached to one end of each wire rotates so they cross, as shown above. The wires close together, gripping the end of the payload shaft. They untwist the opposite way to let go.

## MMU

Both of the astronaut builders are wearing battery-powered Manned Manoeuvring Units, MMUs for short, to fly outside. They have knobs to operate 24 small gas jets to control horizontal and vertical movement. You can find out more about this on page 41.

## Satellite repairing

One of the major jobs of a future station will be satellite repair. In 1984 a Shuttle crew successfully repaired a scientific satellite called Solar Maximum Mission. It was built of separate boxes called modules, each containing major parts. Each module could be unbolted and replaced, to make repair easier. The steps below show how a satellite is repaired.

**1** The RMS grabs the satellite, and puts it in the cargo bay.

**2** An astronaut replaces the faulty satellite parts wearing a spacesuit.

**3** The RMS puts the repaired satellite back into orbit.

**2** The suit is put on in an airlock, where it is stored in two parts – trousers and top, each made up of several layers of different material. Its life-support back-pack carries enough oxygen for seven hours.

▼

Metal rings lock suit together.

Headphones

Display pack

Microphone

**3** There is a soft cap with microphone and headphones, for talking to other crew members and to ground control. A chest pack contains a computer that monitors the workings of the suit all the time. Astronauts can check its display.

**4** Lastly there are gloves that lock onto the suit, and a helmet with a protective plastic visor.

Helmet locks onto suit here.

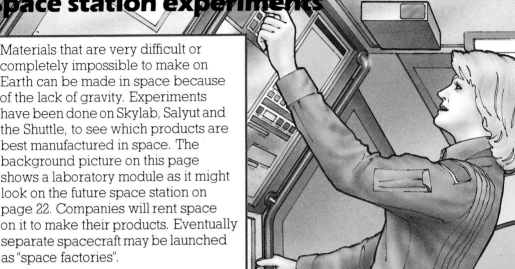

Materials that are very difficult or completely impossible to make on Earth can be made in space because of the lack of gravity. Experiments have been done on Skylab, Salyut and the Shuttle, to see which products are best manufactured in space. The background picture on this page shows a laboratory module as it might look on the future space station on page 22. Companies will rent space on it to make their products. Eventually separate spacecraft may be launched as "space factories".

## Growing crystals

Crystals are sometimes grown on Earth by passing an electric current through a hot solution, so that particles of crystal material separate from the solution and gather together. But the heat causes convection – movements of particles in a warm gas or liquid. This can stop the crystal material separating easily and gathering together evenly. Impurities may also drift into the growing crystal. In space there is no convection, and perfect crystals can be grown for use as chips in electronic circuits. Crystals grown on Earth sometimes turn out to be imperfect, causing electrical short-circuits.

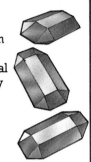

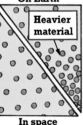

On Earth

Heavier material

In space

## Making alloys

In industry different molten metals are mixed together to make alloys. Alloys are mixtures of metals that are stronger, lighter or longer-lasting than the separate metals. The metals are mixed when molten, but on Earth if two liquid materials of different weights are mixed, the heavier material is pulled down by gravity, and tends to settle at the bottom. In space this doesn't happen, as shown on the left, so new alloys can be made.

## Making medicines

In space some useful biological products can be separated out from living cells in the same way as crystal material, when on Earth convection currents spoil the process. The new materials are used in medicines. For instance, different kinds of kidney cells have been separated to get a substance that dissolves blood clots.

## Perfect lenses

Perfect space bubbles blown from a straw.

In space, liquid floats in a perfect sphere, held together only by surface tension, which acts as the liquid's "skin". The Skylab crew experimented a lot with water. They found that water could be stretched into a sheet which bowed to form a lens perfect in thickness and shape. Experiments to make perfect lenses in the same way from liquid glass are now being done in space.

## First space product

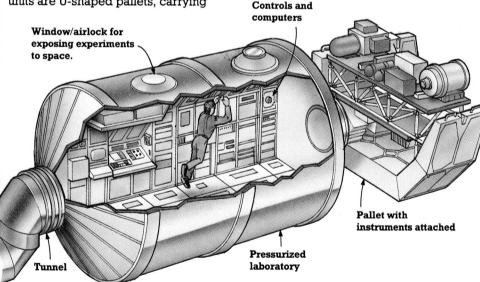

Latex spheres made on Earth vary in size.    In space they are the same size.

The first space product ever to be sold on Earth were tiny perfect spheres made of latex. These would be pulled out of shape by gravity if made on Earth. They are used as tiny rulers to measure objects under a microscope, so need to be a standard size.

## Spacelab

Spacelab is the world's first reusable space laboratory, built by ten European countries. It can be carried in a Shuttle cargo bay. One of its units is a pressurized cylinder-shaped laboratory, carrying experiment racks, work benches and computers to process data. The other units are U-shaped pallets, carrying telescopes and experiments which need to be open to space. The pallets can be fitted into the cargo bay with or without the laboratory. The crew enter the laboratory through a tunnel from the mid-deck of the Shuttle.

Window/airlock for exposing experiments to space.

Controls and computers

Pallet with instruments attached

Tunnel

Pressurized laboratory

## Inside the lab

On board Spacelab there are facilities for making new materials like medicines or alloys, for studying Earth and space, and for analysing the reaction of people and animals to life in space. Before re-entry the crew leave Spacelab and close down the tunnel. But they make sure all the animals are safely in their Spacelab cages and have enough food and water to last until the Shuttle has landed. After each mission the lab can be fitted out with new experiments.

**21**

# Future space stations

Large permanent space stations are the next phase of space exploration. They will act as space observatories and as space factories for making products such as crystals and metal alloys. They will be used for satellite repair and as staging posts for other spacecraft. Although stations will eventually be continuously manned, many of their functions will be performed by automatic robot-like machines. The station shown in the large picture on this page is being designed by America, in partnership with many other countries, for the 1990s. It will be built piece by piece in space by Space Shuttle astronauts.

## Station design

The space station will probably be a "power tower" construction, which is a long spine of interconnecting beams. Cooling systems, electrical power supply and computer data links will run along the length of the spine.

Below is a close-up of some of the modules that will be attached to one end of the beam structure.

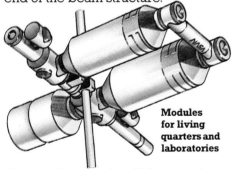

Modules for living quarters and laboratories

They will be used as living quarters, laboratories, payload repair bays, and for storing equipment. There will also be large solar cell arrays on the structure to supply power, together with antennas, space radiators for cooling, docking ports and outside payloads and equipment.

## Unmanned platforms

At least two unmanned platforms will work in conjunction with the station. They will orbit separately, carrying scientific instruments. They will be the world's first permanent satellites, since every part will be renewable in space. One will be in polar orbit, and the other will orbit alongside the station.

Solar arrays

Storage module

Scientific payloads mounted outside

Living and working areas inside spheres

Docking port

## A Russian future station

The USSR is considering a permanent space station, to act as an observatory. It may be made up of cylinders with spheres on each end. The whole station would rotate about the central axis, to give an artificial gravity effect inside. It may be supplied by "astro-taxis" (Shuttle-type vehicles).

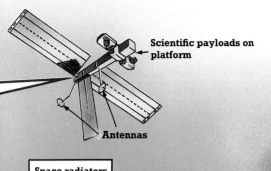

Scientific payloads on platform

Antennas

Space radiators

Communications antenna

Living, laboratory and equipment modules

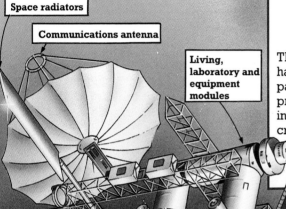

RMS

Payload servicing module

## Payload servicing module

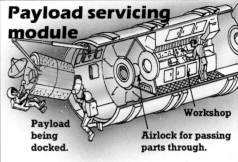

Payload being docked.

Workshop

Airlock for passing parts through.

The payload servicing module will be a hangar for repairing and servicing payloads such as satellites. It will have a pressurized workshop, where individual parts are serviced by the crew. A small airlock will attach it to an unpressurized section where satellites will be parked.

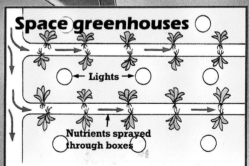

Shuttle Orbiter docked

## Living module

The pressurized living modules will be the most comfortable ever put in space. For the first time astronauts will have a washing machine in space instead of taking their dirty washing home with them. The cutaway picture below shows how the living module may be split into four sections.

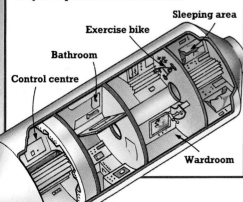

Sleeping area

Exercise bike

Bathroom

Control centre

Wardroom

## Space greenhouses

Lights

Nutrients sprayed through boxes

One of the scientific modules may have a greenhouse area, where vegetables are grown for food and to absorb some of the carbon dioxide breathed out by the crew. One idea, shown below, is for a "plant bank", with racks of plants growing both upwards and downwards towards fluorescent light. Instead of soil, a fine spray of liquid nutrients from a central pipe system circulates round the roots.

**23**

# Return to Earth

Spacecraft re-enter Earth's atmosphere at high speed, overcoming the air's resistance, called drag (see p.10). The air molecules rub against the craft as it falls, shown below, causing friction which produces high temperatures.

The heat caused by re-entry is sometimes used deliberately to burn up unmanned and unwanted craft, such as Progress supply vehicles or Shuttle fuel tanks. Their re-entry path is carefully controlled so that any debris not destroyed by the heat falls harmlessly into the sea. But accidents do occur. Skylab was meant to fall in the Indian Ocean, but some fragments overshot the sea and landed in Australia, luckily causing no damage.

Air resistance

Heat caused by friction

Direction of travel

## Radio blackout

Manned spacecraft have to survive the heat of re-entry to return safely to Earth. Friction heats the air around a spacecraft as well as the ship itself, making a red-hot shield which blocks radio waves to and from the ground for about ten minutes. The spacecraft makes a glowing streak across the sky.

A spacecraft re-entering Earth's atmosphere.

As the craft is slowed down by the atmospheric drag, the heating lessens, and radio communications can resume. The heating effect is minimized by entering the atmosphere at a certain angle, which varies according to each spacecraft.

## Heat shields

Astronauts are protected from re-entry heat by a shield on the outer skin of their ship. The Russian Soyuz and US Apollo craft were not reusable so they were both protected by an "ablative" heat shield, which means it slowly burns away during re-entry.

The reusable Shuttle Orbiter's nose and wing edges, exposed to the highest temperatures on re-entry, are covered with resistant carbon material which doesn't burn away. Black ceramic tiles cover the underside of the body, the front edge of the tail fin and round the windows. Less heat-resistant white tiles cover other parts of the body. Both kinds are made from silica fibres; the difference is in the chemicals used in their tough coatings. The rest of the Shuttle is protected by a silicon felt blanket.

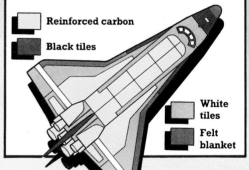

Reinforced carbon

Black tiles

White tiles

Felt blanket

## Descent of Apollo

The Apollo Command Module ferried crew to and from Skylab. When it was ready to return to Earth its engines were fired to slow it down and put it in the right path for re-entry, turning to travel heat shield first. It could skim the top of the atmosphere to further reduce its speed before re-entry. It fell through the atmosphere, slowed by the drag until small parachutes opened at a height of 7,620m (25,000ft). At 4,572m (15,000ft) its three main parachutes opened to lower it gently to the sea, where it was recovered. Soyuz and Apollo descents are similar although Soyuz craft usually touch down

# Shuttle descent

The Shuttle travels a distance of 8,000km (4,971 miles), half-way round the world, from its orbit to its landing site. It is controlled automatically during descent, but is constantly monitored by the pilot.

During landing an autopilot is used, like those in ordinary aircraft. Computers check the flight pattern and relay speed and direction commands. The stages below show a Shuttle descent.

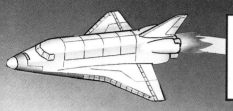

1 An hour before touchdown the Orbiter is turned to face tail-first in its orbit. Manoeuvring engines fire for a couple of minutes to slow it down. This is called "de-orbit burn". The Orbiter turns to face nose-first again as it falls.

2 The orbiter enters the atmosphere at 28,000kph (17,000 mph), at a height of 120km (75 miles). It has a 13 minute radio blackout.

3 The Orbiter experiences maximum heating, 1,540°C (2,800°F), at a height of 70km (43 miles).

4 Conventional aircraft rudder and wing flaps begin to control the Orbiter. They eventually take over from the rocket thrusters so that the Orbiter becomes a very large and fast glider with no power.

on land by firing rockets just before landing to slow down the craft and reduce the bump. Forces due to deceleration, called g-forces, act on the crews as spacecraft descend. They are pushed down in their seats and feel very heavy.

**Apollo splashdown**

5 At 600m (1,968ft) the Orbiter straightens out ready to land. At 76m (249ft) the landing gear automatically comes out.

6 The wheels come down 11 seconds before touchdown, at a speed of 350kph (217mph), twice as fast as an ordinary airliner.

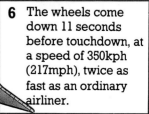

**25**

# Keeping in touch with the ground

All spacecraft must be able to keep in touch with the ground. Communications are sent to and from them by antennas, which are aerials which transmit and receive radio signals.

Signals about an unmanned satellite's internal functions and its position are sent to the ground by a command antenna, which then receives orders for remote controlled corrections (see page 41).

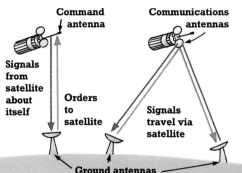

**Command antenna**

**Signals from satellite about itself**

**Orders to satellite**

**Communications antennas**

**Signals travel via satellite**

**Ground antennas**

Communications satellites also have other antennas for relaying radio and TV signals, either in one direction at a time, or back and forth simultaneously, depending on the antenna used.

## Ground stations

Earth installations that receive or send satellite signals are called ground or Earth stations. They have an antenna and equipment to process the signals. They can be large, for satellite or space station control, or small home communications receivers, as shown below. Any ground station must be in direct "line-of-sight" with a satellite. The antenna points in the same direction all the time for geostationary satellites, but must move automatically to track satellites in other orbits.

## Microwaves

Information is sent to and from satellites as microwave signals, a narrow radio beam which spreads out as it travels, like a torch beam. Satellites send microwave signals at different frequencies within a certain limit, just as radio stations use different frequencies within a waveband to carry separate programme channels.

The beams are called "carriers", because they carry information, sometimes in digital form, which means pulses of "on" and "off" signals. These are later converted back into understandable form on Earth. Thousands of digital telephone signals are sent on one carrier. One TV channel, usually sent as a continuous electrical signal (analogue), takes up as much frequency space as thousands of calls.

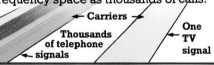

← Carriers →

**Thousands of telephone signals**

One TV signal

## Transponders

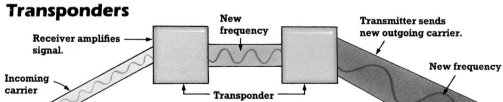

Receiver amplifies signal.

New frequency

Transmitter sends new outgoing carrier.

Incoming carrier

New frequency

Transponder

Communications satellites have several transponders. A transponder is a combination of a receiver and transmitter. The receiver collects, amplifies, and changes the frequency of the faint carrier

signal from Earth. The information on the incoming carrier is then transferred to another carrier signal on a different frequency, before being amplified again and transmitted via an antenna to Earth.

## Footprints

The area covered by a satellite beam on Earth is called its footprint. It can be artificially shaped, by devices on the antennas, to cover large areas such as whole countries, or changed to a narrow "spot beam" for concentrated transmission to one small area.

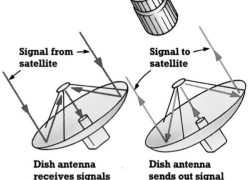

Footprint

## Antennas

Most ground antennas are dish-shaped, as shown on the right. They collect signal carriers and reflect them up to a central place called a focal point. Transmission works the opposite way (small home dishes do not transmit). Dish sizes vary, between about an arm's length for a home TV receiving dish, and the size of buildings for large ground stations. Satellite antennas are not always dish-shaped.

Signal from satellite

Signal to satellite

**Dish antenna receives signals**

**Dish antenna sends out signal**

---

## How home dishes receive TV pictures

Carrier signals are very weak when they reach Earth, so they are amplified several times after being received by a dish. Their frequency is much higher than normal TV or radio signals. It has to be lowered so that it can be amplified properly. The steps below show how a small home dish picks up a TV signal.

**1** Signals are usually reflected by ▶ a plate above the dish down to electronic equipment. In some dishes the signals go straight to equipment mounted at the focal point.

Reflecting plate

**2** An instrument called a ▶ feedhorn gathers up the signals reflected by the dish and sends them to an electronic device called a low noise amplifier (LNA).

LNA →

Feedhorn

Downconverter

**3** Inside the LNA the tiny satellite signal is amplified about 100,000 times. It is further amplified in another device called a downconverter, which lowers the signal frequency too.

**4** The signal is sent by cable to ▶ the receiver, inside a nearby building. It is a box with dials, for selecting information from the carrier, such as a TV channel.

Receiver

TV picture and → sound

**5** Inside the receiver the signal is amplified and again lowered in frequency. The receiver extracts sound and picture information to power the TV.

# Communications satellites

Communications satellites, comsats for short, relay all kinds of messages around the world, often between areas so far apart that an ordinary wire link-up would be very difficult. A comsat is like a broadcasting tower in space – an automatic relay station that transmits to its footprint area.

Most comsats use geostationary orbit, so that they stay above the same point on Earth. They make it possible to watch live transmissions of events like the Olympics. They link countries' telephone systems directly and cheaply. Much financial business is conducted at high speed via comsats, often in the form of computer data or pictures of documents. Comsats are also used to transmit educational material to remote areas. For instance, Indonesia, a nation made up of many isolated islands, uses its Palapa satellites to connect islanders with one teacher in a central location.

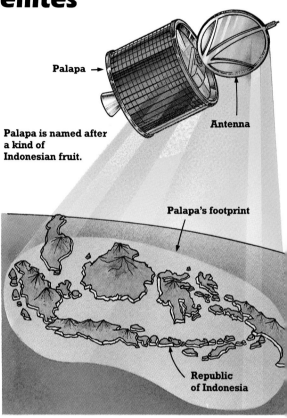

**Palapa**

**Antenna**

Palapa is named after a kind of Indonesian fruit.

**Palapa's footprint**

**Republic of Indonesia**

## A long-distance phone-call

The steps below show how Comsats transmit telephone calls between continents. The signals travel between telephones via a satellite in a second or so.

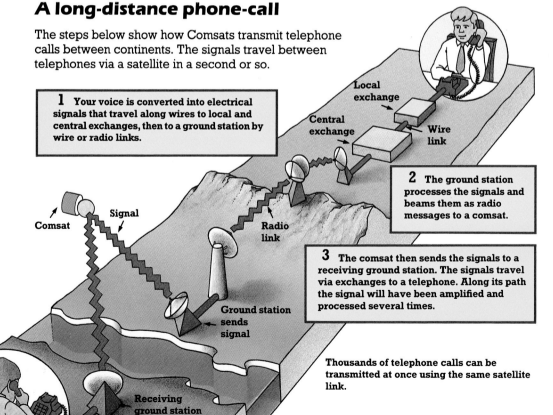

**1** Your voice is converted into electrical signals that travel along wires to local and central exchanges, then to a ground station by wire or radio links.

**Local exchange**

**Central exchange**

**Wire link**

**2** The ground station processes the signals and beams them as radio messages to a comsat.

**Comsat**

**Signal**

**Radio link**

**3** The comsat then sends the signals to a receiving ground station. The signals travel via exchanges to a telephone. Along its path the signal will have been amplified and processed several times.

**Ground station sends signal**

**Receiving ground station**

Thousands of telephone calls can be transmitted at once using the same satellite link.

## Intelsat

Intelsat is a group of nations owning a series of international comsats in geostationary orbit. These transmit between ground stations owned by the member countries. The picture on the right shows how three Intelsat satellites cover most of the world.

Another comsat system is the Russian Molniya satellites, which are in a high eccentric orbit, shown on page 11. Three Molniyas are in the same orbit so that as one disappears below the horizon another appears above the opposite horizon. The ground station dishes for this system have to move automatically to track the satellites as they move around their orbit.

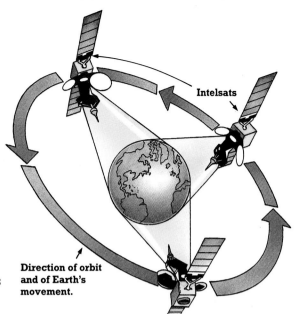

Intelsats

Direction of orbit and of Earth's movement.

## Domestic comsats

Live TV pictures usually travel between countries via satellites, then through a normal TV transmission network to home sets. But large countries use their own domestic satellites, transmitting national TV programmes straight to small ground stations serving remote local communities. The signals are then beamed from a TV tower, or run to local houses by a cable. TV companies rent channel space on domestic satellites and beam their own programmes to ground stations. The signals are then run through cables to the TV sets of nearby customers.

## Direct broadcast satellites (DBS)

Small dish aerials on buildings or in gardens can pick up comsat signals directly if they are within range of a satellite footprint. This is called direct satellite broadcasting, and means that TV can be transmitted cheaply to a wide area without the need for lots of ground stations. The dishes must point directly at the correct point above the Equator.

In some countries anyone can own a receiving system to pick up satellite signals. In other countries people need a licence to set up a ground station. In the future this will change, as more services become available around the world, transmitted through special DBS systems that send a strong signal for reception by small dishes. Soon small receiving antennas will become a common sight, on house rooves or in gardens.

Antenna

## Signals across space

There are plans for satellites to relay signals directly to each other, so that they can transmit more quickly over great distances. The TDRS satellite now links the Shuttle to Mission Control in the USA, when the Shuttle is round the other side of the world, and it sometimes links the Landsat Earth resources satellite to Earth. In the future satellites will communicate with each other via laser beams (see page 42).

# Images of Earth

Over the next four pages you can find out about unmanned "remote sensing" satellites, which carry instruments to survey the Earth's surface and atmosphere. The data received from these is transmitted to ground stations, where computers process it into information or images. Pictures built up electronically from data are really images rather than photographs, because they are not recorded on photographic film.

## Weather

Meteorological satellites (metsats) provide cloud images and temperature and moisture measurements, which help scientists to study and predict the weather. They also collect and relay data from weather stations such as ships.

## Earth resources

Earth resources satellites survey wide areas of the Earth's surface quickly and repeatedly, providing images which show up many different landscape features. The images are put to many uses, shown in the panel on the far right.

## Remote sensing orbits

A network of five geostationary metsats provides a weather-watch for the world, each one viewing about a quarter of the Earth's surface, continously recording weather changes.

Other metsats and most Earth resources satellites circle the Earth in low polar orbit, covering almost the whole of its surface after many orbits. For example, the Landsat Earth resources satellite orbits 14 times a day, seeing all of the Earth, except an area round the Poles, after 18 days (251 orbits). Its orbit is at an angle of about 10° to a truly polar orbit. This means it remains in line with the Sun shining on Earth and it always gathers its images in sunlight. The images are recorded at the same time of day for each place. This orbit is called "Sun-synchronous".

The picture below shows how remote sensing satellites orbit the Earth.

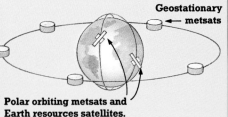

Geostationary metsats

Polar orbiting metsats and Earth resources satellites.

## Metsat picture

The image of the Earth below is from data sent back by Meteosat, one of the five geostationary metsats. New picture data is transmitted every 30 minutes from each metsat, and can be picked up by anyone with the right sort of antenna and equipment to convert the signals into a picture. You can see a Landsat picture on page 33.

# Landsat

The picture below shows a Landsat Earth resources satellite. It carries two detecting instruments. One is called a Multi-spectral scanner and can register anything on the Earth's surface over 80 metres (262ft) wide. The other is called a Thematic Mapper. It can pick out areas over 30 metres (98ft) wide. The information is transmitted directly down to ground stations or via the TDRS communications satellite. The French Earth resources satellite called SPOT, launched in 1985, can register even smaller areas, down to 10 metres (33') wide. You can find out how detecting instruments work on the next page.

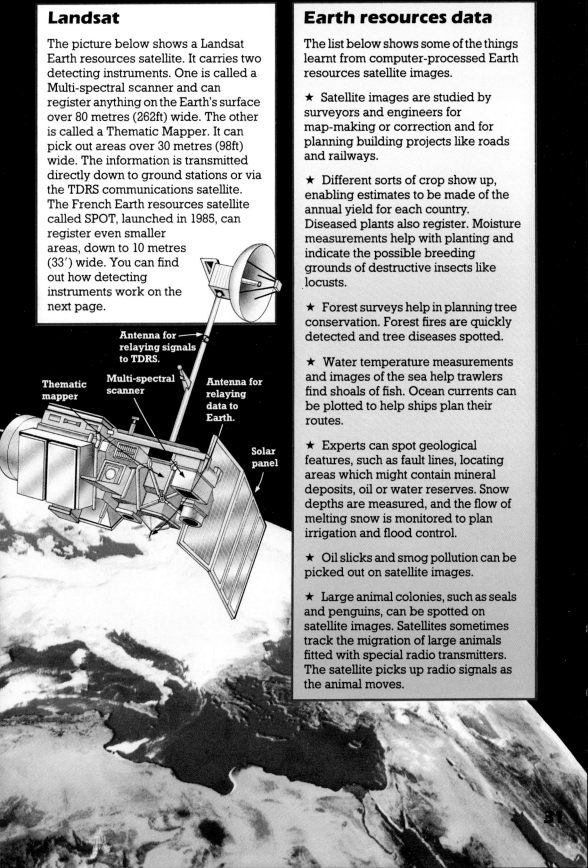

Antenna for relaying signals to TDRS.

Thematic mapper

Multi-spectral scanner

Antenna for relaying data to Earth.

Solar panel

# Earth resources data

The list below shows some of the things learnt from computer-processed Earth resources satellite images.

★ Satellite images are studied by surveyors and engineers for map-making or correction and for planning building projects like roads and railways.

★ Different sorts of crop show up, enabling estimates to be made of the annual yield for each country. Diseased plants also register. Moisture measurements help with planting and indicate the possible breeding grounds of destructive insects like locusts.

★ Forest surveys help in planning tree conservation. Forest fires are quickly detected and tree diseases spotted.

★ Water temperature measurements and images of the sea help trawlers find shoals of fish. Ocean currents can be plotted to help ships plan their routes.

★ Experts can spot geological features, such as fault lines, locating areas which might contain mineral deposits, oil or water reserves. Snow depths are measured, and the flow of melting snow is monitored to plan irrigation and flood control.

★ Oil slicks and smog pollution can be picked out on satellite images.

★ Large animal colonies, such as seals and penguins, can be spotted on satellite images. Satellites sometimes track the migration of large animals fitted with special radio transmitters. The satellite picks up radio signals as the animal moves.

# More about images of Earth

All objects emit and reflect radiation. Remote sensing means detecting and measuring this radiation from a distance. Ordinary cameras work in this way, picking up visible light radiation from objects through a lens and recording it on light-sensitive film. Satellite remote sensing instruments record images and other information as electrical signals, which are sent back to Earth as radio messages. They can be either TV cameras, which pick up visible light, or radiometers, instruments with detectors sensitive to different kinds of radiation. Radiometer measurements are used to produce computer-processed Earth images like the picture on the opposite page.

## Electromagnetic radiation

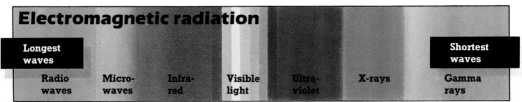

| Longest waves | | | | | | Shortest waves |
|---|---|---|---|---|---|---|
| Radio waves | Micro-waves | Infra-red | Visible light | Ultra-violet | X-rays | Gamma rays |

The light that you see (visible light) is a small part of a wide range of radiation called electromagnetic radiation. A radiometer detects and measures this radiation. The whole radiation range (spectrum) is shown above (not to scale).

Radiation is said to travel in invisible "waves", and different types are identified by the length of these waves. Radiometer detectors measure a single wavelength, or a small group of wavelengths called a "band". Most radiometers have several detectors, measuring several different bands at once. For Earth resources and metsats these bands are usually in the infra-red part of the spectrum.

## Signatures

Every object emits radiation and reflects some of the radiation that falls on it from other sources. But different objects emit and reflect different amounts of each wavelength. The quantity of each wavelength of radiation emitted from an object is called its "signature", which identifies it like a fingerprint. For example, different species of plants reflect different amounts of each wavelength in the infra-red band, so different crops can be identified on images. Heat is infra-red radiation. So radiometers sensitive to radiation in the infra-red band width are used to measure the temperature of land, sea and clouds.

## How a radiometer works

A radiometer has many detectors, each fitted with a filter which blocks out all but the wavelength or band of radiation the detector measures. The steps below show how radiometers detect radiation.

**Scanning mirror**

**Secondary mirror**

← Radiation from Earth

**Primary mirror**

**Filters and detectors**

**Electrical signals sent to satellite's recording and relaying system.**

**2** Radiation from the focused image is measured by the array of detectors. Some must be kept cool in order to work.

**3** The radiation makes the detectors emit electrical signals, which are recorded. The satellite later transmits them to Earth.

**1** The radiation from the scene below the satellite is collected by mirrors and focused to form an image.

# How a radiometer scans

Satellites scan the ground in a series of strips, put together to make up a complete image. Polar orbiting satellites use a scanning mirror in front of the other focusing mirrors. It moves to and fro to reflect radiation into the radiometer from different parts of a strip across the satellite path. Geostationary satellites use a different mirror arrangement to scan strips.

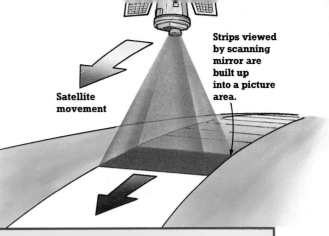

Satellite movement

Strips viewed by scanning mirror are built up into a picture area.

## Computer processing

Satellite radiometer measurements are processed by computers on Earth to produce useful images. A computer can enhance an image using one band of radiation by increasing the contrast between different picture areas.

It can also add false colours to make particular features show up clearly. For instance, oil slicks are not easy to spot against water unless the computer shows areas with a signature indicating oil in a different colour. Images from different radiation bands can be combined for a highly detailed picture.

## A satellite picture

This is a satellite picture of the Humber Estuary, in England, from Landsat Thematic Mapper data. A computer has processed the picture to show different areas in different colours.

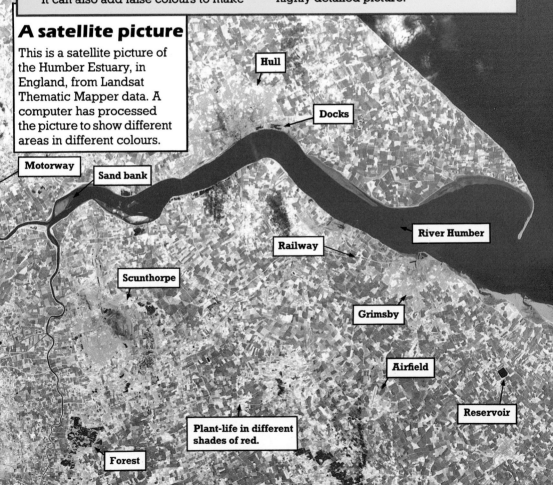

Hull

Docks

Motorway

Sand bank

River Humber

Railway

Scunthorpe

Grimsby

Airfield

Reservoir

Plant-life in different shades of red.

Forest

# Scientific satellites

Scientific satellites have remote sensing instruments on board which either study Earth's environment or the solar system, or look further away into deep space. They act as observation posts above the atmosphere, a moving ocean of air, cloud and dust that blocks the view from Earth. Ordinary light given out by stars and galaxies does not reach Earth telescopes clearly. Satellites above the atmosphere receive much clearer pictures, which are relayed to Earth.

Visible light from many bodies in space cannot be detected because they are so far away. They do, however, give out different kinds of radiation, which is especially strong when a violent event happens, such as a star explosion or collision. These radiation sources can only be pinpointed by astronomical satellites, controlled from Earth to look at any part of space.

## Studying the Sun

The Sun is the nearest star to Earth and it gives astronomers an idea of how stars work in general. Scientists also study the Sun's effect on Earth's environment. Explosions of gas on the Sun's surface, called solar flares, affect Earth's weather patterns and radio broadcasts. Scientific satellites and space station crews take measurements and record activity on the Sun's surface.

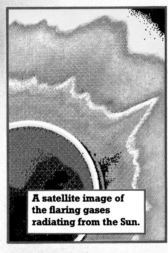

A satellite image of the flaring gases radiating from the Sun.

## Space near Earth

Early satellites measured dust particles around the Earth to see if they would pose a danger to manned missions. They turned out to be fairly harmless. Satellites now monitor the ozone in the upper atmosphere. It is a kind of oxygen gas shielding Earth from harmful ultra-violet rays. Satellite data shows that the ozone layer may be harmed by man-made pollution.

## Solar wind

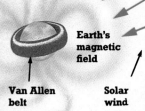

Earth's magnetic field

Van Allen belt

Solar wind

The Sun sends out a constant stream of atomic particles into space, called the solar wind. Some of these particles are trapped by the Earth's magnetic field and form belts of radiation round the Earth called the Van Allen belts, discovered by a satellite. Other satellites have shown that the solar wind blows the Earth's magnetic field into the shape shown above.

## The Space Telescope

The Space Telescope launched in 1986, is designed to be lifted out of a Shuttle cargo bay by the RMS arm. Then its two solar cell arrays open automatically and it orbits as an unmanned satellite about 600km (373 miles) above Earth. It should work for 20 years. Astronauts from a Shuttle or permanent space station will visit it every two and a half years to service it, and will bring it back to Earth for a major overhaul every five years. Although there are larger astronomical telescopes on Earth, it can see objects 50 times fainter or seven times further away than any built so far.

# Discoveries in space

Observation of space gives scientists an idea of how the Universe evolved. The radiation satellites detect has often taken an extremely long time to reach Earth, and is the result of events such as star explosions that happened billions of years ago, when the Universe was young.

Satellites have found X-ray sources in space which may be black holes – objects with a force of gravity so great that nothing can escape them, not even light. They may be created when a huge star collapses. Gases from nearby stars swirl into the hole, giving out the X-rays.

One exciting discovery made from satellite data is a ring of material round a nearby star called Vega. This could be a solar system, the first evidence of planets outside our own solar system.

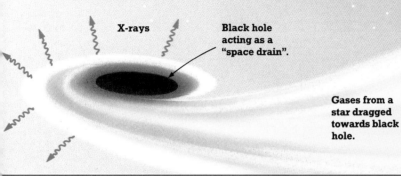

X-rays

Black hole acting as a "space drain".

Gases from a star dragged towards black hole.

# How it works

The picture on the right shows how the telescope collects electromagnetic radiation from space. It works in the same way as ground telescopes. A large primary mirror reflects the rays onto a small secondary mirror in front of it. The small mirror sends them back through a hole in the large mirror, to a range of detectors that register ultra-violet, infra-red and visible light rays. The data collected is relayed to computers on Earth for processing, and then made available to astronomers.

**The telescope points with such accuracy that it could focus on a small coin in Los Angeles from San Francisco 700km (435 miles) away.**

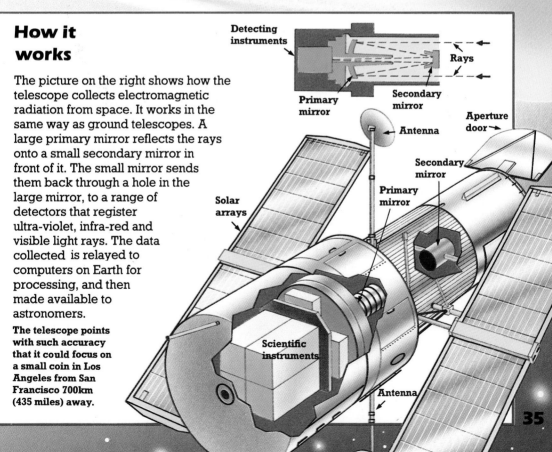

Detecting instruments

Rays

Primary mirror

Secondary mirror

Aperture door

Antenna

Secondary mirror

Primary mirror

Solar arrays

Scientific instruments

Antenna

# Navigation satellites

For centuries sailors have plotted their position and course by observing bright stars. Navigation satellites act as man-made stars, by sending down radio signals giving their position in space and the correct time. Using the signals from four satellites sailors can calculate their own position on Earth. New improved navigation satellite systems are now being planned and tested by Russia, America and Europe to give continuous and amazingly accurate information for ships and aircraft. You can find out about a typical new system below.

## Navstar

The US Global Positioning System (GPS) is now being built and tested for use by many people around the world. It uses 18 Navstar satellites. They will be launched into six different circular orbits 20,000km (12,428 miles) high. They are in a high orbit partly to prevent possible enemy attacks. They could be used to guide armies or missiles to their target, so they are protected against deliberate electronic jamming of their systems.

The picture on the right shows the Navstar satellites spread round six orbits. Each Navstar takes 12 hours to circle the Earth; four Navstars can be seen at any time from anywhere on Earth.

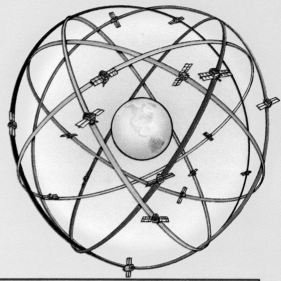

## How Navstar works

**Technician (to same scale)**

**Navstar before launch**

**Antennas**

The picture on the left shows a Navstar. It is very large and complicated, with over 33,000 parts. Each Navstar carries three atomic clocks, accurate to one second in 30,000 years. They continuously transmit signals on their position in orbit and the time. Users on Earth have equipment which receives signals from the four Navstars in view and calculates the ground position to an accuracy of up to 16m (52ft). This includes the vertical as well as the horizontal position for aircraft. Speed can be worked out, too, to an accuracy of 0.1m/sec (.3ft/sec). The picture below shows Navstars in use.

Vehicles can have an electronic speaking map to receive satellite signals, and work out their position.

Navstars are monitored by ground stations to make sure they are in the right orbit.

Soldiers or even ordinary hikers can carry a lightweight "man-pack" to receive Navstar signals.

Their position is corrected by a central control station, which also checks their atomic clocks.

# Military satellites

Many satellites have military uses too. Comsats are used to keep armies and military bases in touch, and to pick up signals from secret agents with transmitters, or automatic ground spying equipment. Their messages are scrambled so that only some receivers can decode them. Metsats predict the weather for army exercises, and tell military planners when an area will be clear of cloud, so that a spy satellite can film it. Countries are very secretive about their military satellites. Even civilian satellites are sometimes secretly fitted with small extra devices for military use.

## Spy photography

Recovery capsule jettisoned.

Recovery by aircraft

Capsule re-entry

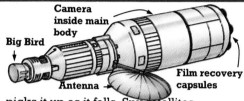

Camera inside main body

Big Bird

Antenna

Film recovery capsules

Satellites can spy on countries without being harmed. Some use real film because it provides a more detailed image than TV pictures transmitted by electrical signal. They jettison the film in a heatproof capsule, shown in the picture above. The capsule's re-entry path is carefully planned, and an aeroplane picks it up as it falls. Spy satellites sometimes carry infra-red sensors that transmit images in digital form. The spy satellite above is called Big Bird. It has a camera so good that its photographs show up people on the ground from over 161km (100 miles) up. It carries recovery capsules on board.

## Radar spy satellites

Radar satellites keep watch on moving targets, like warships. One kind is nuclear-powered, generating enough electricity to drive a very powerful radar (see page 38 for more about satellite nuclear power). After its mission a radio signal from the ground orders the satellite to split into pieces. The nuclear section has its own rocket motor to boost it into high orbit, where it should stay for 600 years.

Other types of spy satellite carry radio receivers to listen in to enemy radio and radar signals. They are called "ferrets".

## Laser weapons

"Killer" satellites blow themselves up near a target in space to destroy it. New killer satellites are being developed with the capacity to destroy other satellites or missiles with laser beams – powerful streams of very concentrated light energy. Satellites can also be destroyed by infra-red heat seeking missiles launched by planes. Experiments are going on to produce "dark satellites", which don't give out much light or heat to detect.

## Early warning

Early warning satellites carry infra-red sensors to detect the hot exhaust of a nuclear missile. They carry equipment to transmit photos of the missiles at the same time, to prove the satellite has not made an error. They can detect a missile within seconds of ignition. Equipment for early warning can be fitted to ordinary military or civilian satellites.

# Satellite power

All the systems on board a satellite or space station need electrical power to operate. This power must be provided on board the satellite; it is very difficult to beam it from Earth.

Most satellites have solar cells which convert the Sun's radiation into electrical energy. Some carry nuclear or chemical fuels which can be converted into electricity. Power from energy sources is stored in a battery and supplied to parts when needed.

## How solar cells work

Most satellites and space stations in Earth orbit use solar cells called photovoltaic cells. They are made from silicon, with an impurity added to alter its ability to conduct electricity, making it a semi-conductor.

A very thin top layer of the silicon is treated with another sort of impurity to make it a different type of semi-conductor. When light falls on the top surface of the cell an electrical voltage is produced between the two types of semi-conductor, as shown on the right. Metal contacts on the top and bottom of the cell conduct the current to storage batteries.

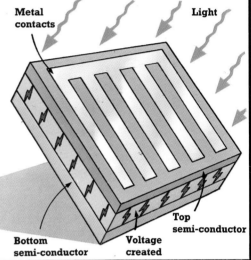

Metal contacts

Light

Bottom semi-conductor

Voltage created

Top semi-conductor

## Solar arrays

A single cell only provides a tiny amount of electricity, so hundreds are connected up to provide a larger supply. They are welded together using a very accurate robot welder, as shown below, to make a sheet called a solar array.

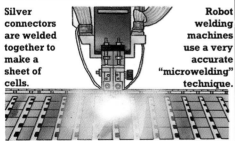

Silver connectors are welded together to make a sheet of cells.

Robot welding machines use a very accurate "microwelding" technique.

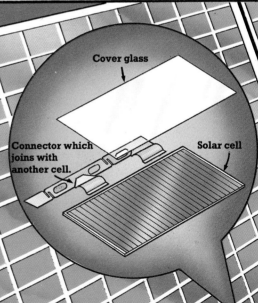

Cover glass

Connector which joins with another cell.

Solar cell

The sheets are placed either round a satellite body or on panels that extend like wings. If the cells are around a spacecraft body, on spinning satellites for example, some cells will always be in shadow. So many extra cells are needed to keep the satellite going.

# A solar-powered satellite

The picture below shows a comsat called HS 394. It has a spinning body covered in solar cells and solar cell "wings" spanning 35 metres (115ft) right across.

The wings generate 4000 watts of electricity continuously for the communications equipment, enough to power four bars of an electric fire. The solar array on the body provides 400 watts for the housekeeping functions.

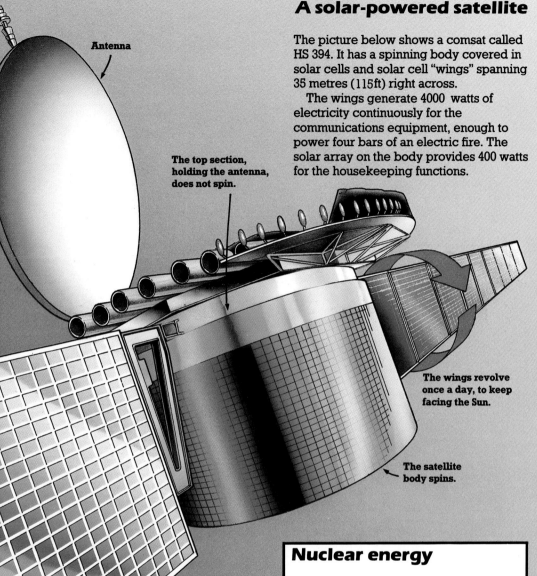

**Antenna**

**The top section, holding the antenna, does not spin.**

**The wings revolve once a day, to keep facing the Sun.**

**The satellite body spins.**

## Fuel cells

Fuel cells convert chemical energy into electrical energy, using chemical reactions in which electrical charges are released. The Shuttle uses fuel cells in which oxygen and hydrogen, from storage tanks, are combined to make water, releasing electrical energy as they do so.

Chemical fuels are used up quickly, so they cannot be used on satellites designed to operate for many years.

## Nuclear energy

On some satellites nuclear fuel is used to produce heat which is then converted to electricity. This fuel gives out energy as it gradually loses its radioactivity.

There are problems with this type of fuel. Even though the satellite may be put into a very high orbit it could still crash to Earth, posing great danger to life. In 1982 a part of a Russian nuclear-powered satellite crashed in a remote area of Canada, but luckily caused no damage.

Few satellites in Earth orbit are nuclear powered because of the danger involved. But space probes journeying to the outer solar system use nuclear power successfully.

# Building satellites

All satellites are built to operate reliably during their lifetime, which can be up to ten years. Occasionally they do go wrong and those in low orbit can sometimes be repaired by the Shuttle crew. Every satellite component must be built to withstand acceleration and vibration during launch. Once in orbit some satellite parts need to be adequately shielded from space debris and the Sun's radiation.

Satellite designers need to take these problems into account, and also make sure that every part fits together so that the satellite is the right size and weight, balances properly, points the right way, and maintains the right temperature.

## Shape and weight

A satellite must be light enough, including the fuel it carries, for a launch vehicle to send it into the correct orbit. It must also be able to fold down to fit into a rocket nosecone or a Shuttle cargo bay. The pictures below show different ways satellite parts are stowed. They unfold automatically after launch.

Solar cell panels can be folded at the sides of the satellite.

... or they can be wrapped around the satellite body.

Two shells of solar cells can be telescoped together.

The bottom shell comes down after launch. Antennas unfold.

## Building materials

The materials used to build a satellite must be light, but strong enough to withstand the stresses of launch. Carbon fibre and aluminium are often used. Aluminium is strengthened by being made in special forms, such as honeycomb sheets (shown below). These are used to support solar panels. Titanium is a rare metal that is very strong at high temperatures. It is used to make extra-tough bolts on spacecraft.

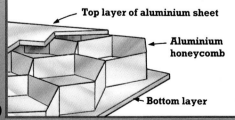

Top layer of aluminium sheet

Aluminium honeycomb

Bottom layer

## Temperature

The side of a satellite exposed to sunlight gets very hot. But the part in shadow gets very cold. Insulating blankets are fitted to the cold side and reflective mirrors to the hot side. Some parts, such as batteries, produce unwanted heat as they work. They must be placed so it radiates into space. Paints and surface finishes absorb and radiate heat differently. The right mixture of polished, rough or metallic surfaces, such as gold foil, helps control temperature.

## Testing

Every satellite part is tested in a simulated space environment, before and after they are assembled. They are exposed to a vacuum, radiation, heat, vibration, acceleration and shock. Satellites are built in special clean chambers where the air that enters is thoroughly filtered and technicians wear hygienic clothes, like hospital surgeons. A tiny speck of dust could stop a part working.

Crucial components are sometimes duplicated, so that if one fails another automatically takes over. Computers are used to make complicated calculations and design drawings during manufacture.

# Pointing satellites

Small forces such as the solar wind tend to push satellites out of their correct orbit. Ground stations track each satellite and computers calculate any changes needed. "Station keeping" commands are then sent via the satellite's command antenna to its on-board propulsion system, which fires to correct the orbit.

An "attitude control" system keeps a satellite's body, and special parts like antennas, pointing in the right direction. It relies on sensors that react to changes in direction by sending out electrical "error" signals. On-board circuitry processes them and sends corrective commands to equipment which turns the satellite.

## Stabilizing

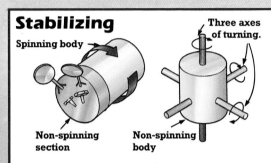

Spinning body

Three axes of turning.

Non-spinning section

Non-spinning body

Satellites are stabilized to keep them pointing the right way. One method is to keep a satellite spinning continuously about its central axis, as shown above. This helps it resist any small forces. There is usually a non-spinning top section holding equipment such as antennas that need to point at Earth.

"Three-axis stabilization" is used by non-spinning satellites. They correct their position by turning only when needed about any one of three axes, shown above. "Pointing" satellites, usually scientific ones, are similar to three-axis stabilized satellites. However, they are turned on command so that their instruments point in the required direction.

## Sensors

Satellites use different kinds of sensors to check their position. Optical sensors are usually made up of several light-sensitive detectors. Lenses focus an image of the Sun, or stars, onto them. If a satellite moves the image shifts and the detectors respond.

Another kind of sensor is a gyroscope, a kind of spinning wheel which tilts in a different direction when a satellite turns. A third kind of sensor responds to changes in the strength and direction of the Earth's magnetic field around the satellite.

## Turning a satellite

Satellites are turned to point in the right direction by thrusters, which are small nozzles. When gas is expelled from them in one direction the satellite will turn in the opposite direction, as shown below. MMUs (Manned Manoeuvring Units) work the same way. Try the experiment below, which imitates how thrusters work.

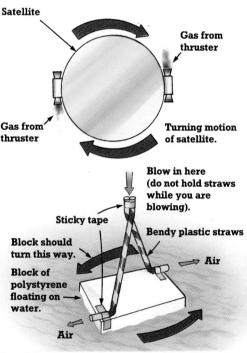

Satellite

Gas from thruster

Gas from thruster

Turning motion of satellite.

Blow in here (do not hold straws while you are blowing).

Sticky tape

Bendy plastic straws

Block should turn this way.

Air

Block of polystyrene floating on water.

Air

Special wheels called inertia wheels can also turn satellites. When the wheel, fixed to a satellite body, turns, the satellite reacts by turning in the opposite direction. The wheels are operated by electric motors activated by the attitude control computer circuits.

**41**

# Space plans

Space science, tested on today's satellites and space stations, is rapidly being developed for future projects, some of them involving huge structures in space as big as cities. There are plans to build in space using materials mined from the Moon and from asteroids (lumps of rock floating in space which may be the building blocks of unformed planets). Some ideas will become reality before the end of the century, but others will only be possible when technology becomes much more advanced.

## Space tethers

**The near future**

A space tether is a strong cable made of strong synthetic material. In the near future the Shuttle will probably take up a satellite into low orbit and release it on the end of a tether. The satellite will swing up high, like a ball swung on the end of a piece of string. When released from the tether, it will only need a small final boost into high orbit. The Shuttle may also dangle a satellite into the atmosphere, so that it will be able to make scientific measurements without being dragged down by gravity.

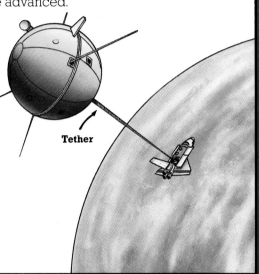

Tether

## Future comsats

**End of 20th century**

The geostationary orbit is becoming very crowded with comsats. There are plans to send up a few very large new kinds of comsat instead of many smaller ones. The picture on the right shows a design for one new type. It is constructed from several antennas joined onto a beam structure, and is called an "antenna farm".

Another plan is to have new large comsats (shown bottom right) orbiting the continents of the world, bouncing signals between each other by laser beam. At the moment, to send a signal a great distance it has to be bounced back and forth between lots of ground stations and satellites. This is not always practical because ground stations may not be sighted along every route.

When comsats relay signals to each other directly communications will be transmitted more efficiently, between two ground stations anywhere in the world.

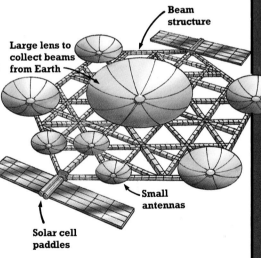

Beam structure

Large lens to collect beams from Earth

Small antennas

Solar cell paddles

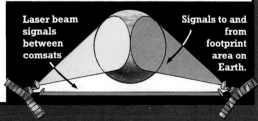

Laser beam signals between comsats

Signals to and from footprint area on Earth.

## Space power stations

The picture on the right shows a giant solar power collecting satellite, that may be built in the next century. It could change sunlight into microwave energy and beam it to a receiving station. It would then be converted into electricity for use in millions of homes.

In the future, enormous satellites like

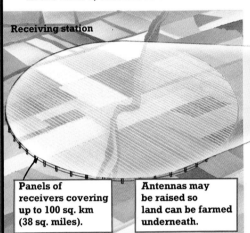

Solar cell collector covering 50 sq. km (19 sq. miles).

Antenna for sending beams to Earth.

Receiving station

Panels of receivers covering up to 100 sq. km (38 sq. miles).

Antennas may be raised so land can be farmed underneath.

these could be built by workers from a Moon colony, using metal processed from Moon rock. But there are still many problems to overcome. The microwave beams could be dangerous to birds or light aircraft flying through them, and they would interfere with radio and radar signals in the beam path.

The distant future

## Space colonies

A long way in the future huge space stations may float far above Earth, out past the Moon. People will live and work there, producing high-quality space products, mining asteroids for metals and growing their own food. They could be ferried from Earth in Shuttle-type vehicles, to "space hotels", and then onward to the colonies. There are many suggestions for different cylinder or wheel-shaped colonies. One is shown on the left. It could accommodate 10,000 people.

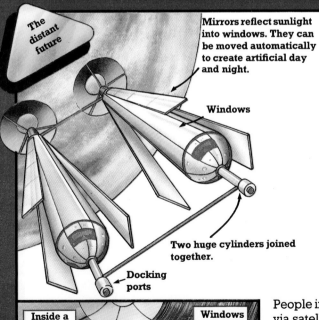

Mirrors reflect sunlight into windows. They can be moved automatically to create artificial day and night.

Windows

Two huge cylinders joined together.

Docking ports

Inside a cylinder

Windows

Landscaped strips

People in colonies will be in touch with Earth via satellites. They may even watch events on Earth, like a football match, converted into a holograph in space, so that the players appear real in front of them. Colonies could be landscaped to look like different parts of the world.

**43**

# Satellite orbit computer program

If you have or can borrow a computer, use this program to put your own imaginary satellites into different orbits. The program launches satellites sideways from a point in space. You choose the altitude (height) of the satellite in km or miles, and its speed in km/sec or miles/sec.

Your computer will give coordinates (points on a graph) at different points of the satellite's path at certain times, taking into account the Earth's gravitational pull at different heights. You then plot these points on graph paper and join them up to make an orbit. The program will also give you a scaled measurement of the Earth's radius, so that you can draw it. The size of the Earth depends on the satellite orbit you choose.

---

This program works on the following computers: Commodore 64, MSX, BBC, VIC-20, Spectrum, Apple, Electron, TRS-80 Colour Computer with extended Basic.

---

## Things you need

Squared graph paper – either 10mm or 1 inch squared (further divided into ¹/₁₀ inches) depending on whether you want the program in metric or imperial measurements. Count each unit the program plots as one of the small squares on the paper. Half a small square is shown on the screen as .5.

Coloured pencils, compasses, rubber.

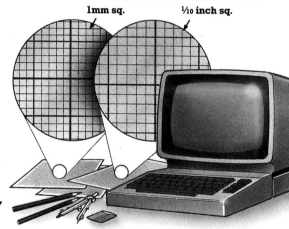

1mm sq.          ¹/₁₀ inch sq.

## What to do

**1** Type in the program. (Change line 10 on the screen if you want to run the program using imperial measurements. The alternative line is shown at the bottom of the program).

**2** Draw a cross on your graph paper, the size shown below. The lines, called axes, should be of equal lengths. Label each axis as shown.

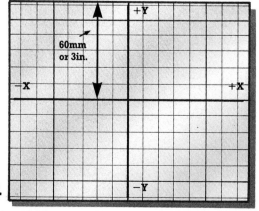

60mm or 3in.

**3** Type RUN (or your computer's word) to start the program.
Type a number for height*.
Press return.
Type a number for a speed*.
Press return.
*See suggestions on opposite page.

**4** Draw a circle of the radius shown on the screen, by hand if it is small (see example below). Colour it in if you like, but make sure you can still see the squares underneath it, you'll need to count them.

**Radius of 6mm (¼ inch).**

**5** Plot the first point in the orbit like this:
The program gives you a number for the X and Y axes. Count the number of small squares along the +X axis, then up the +Y axis. Mark the coordinate with a dot. Press C, then RETURN to continue.

**6** Continue to plot points round the orbit, as shown below. As you move round the program will give you numbers for the −X and −Y axes.

If your satellite is quite high, it is quicker to plot one out of every four or five computer readings. If your satellite goes close to the Earth you need to plot every point. The satellite is going faster at this stage, so each point will be further apart.

**7** Join up the dots you have marked to see the path of the orbit, as shown below. Type S, RETURN, then RUN (or your computer's word) to plot a new orbit on a new graph.

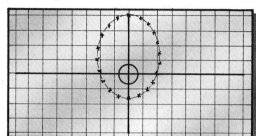

## Suggestions

At a low height your satellite will need to go faster to combat gravity and stay in orbit. If it is going too slowly the program will say "RE=ENTRY", which means your satellite has crashed! This will happen below 200km (124 miles). If you make your satellite go too fast it will go into a huge orbit off the page. Try heights below 40,000km (24,856 miles) and speeds between 11 and 1 km/sec (7 and 0.62 m/sec). You could start off by plotting the orbits below.

Geostationary. Height 36,000km (22,370 miles). Speed 3.1km/sec (1.92 miles/sec). This orbit takes approximately 24 hours.

Eccentric elliptical, like the Russian satellites shown on page 11. Height 40,000km (24,856 miles). Speed 1.5km/sec (0.93 miles/sec). This orbit takes approximately 12 hours.

```
  10 LET U$="KM":LET P$="MM":LET F1=1:LET F2=1
  20 LET ME=6.0E24:LET RE=6.4E6
  30 LET K=3.14159265/180:LET G=6.7E-11
  40 PRINT "STARTING CONDITIONS:"
  50 PRINT "ALTITUDE (";U$;")":INPUT D:LET D=D*1000*F1+RE
  60 PRINT "SPEED (";U$;"/S) ":INPUT V:LET V=V*1000*F1
  70 LET SC=50/D:LET A=90
  80 PRINT:PRINT "DRAW THE EARTH WITH RADIUS ";
  90 PRINT INT(RE*SC*10/F2)/10;" ";P$
 100 LET XS=0:LET YS=D:LET TT=0
 110 LET VX=V:LET VY=0
 120 LET A$="":LET C=0:LET T=(6.28*D/V)/600
 130 LET DS=ABS(XS*XS+YS*YS)
 140 IF SQR(DS)<6.6E6 THEN PRINT "RE-ENTRY":STOP
 150 LET AG=-G*(ME/DS):LET A=(ATN(XS/YS))/K
 160 IF YS<0 THEN LET A=A+180
 170 IF A<0 THEN LET A=A+360
 180 LET AK=A*K
 190 LET VX=VX+T*AG*SIN(AK):LET VY=VY+T*AG*COS(AK)
 200 LET XS=XS+VX*T:LET YS=YS+VY*T
 210 LET TT=TT+T
 220 LET C=C+1:IF C=2 THEN GOSUB 250
 230 IF A$<>"S" THEN GOTO 130
 240 STOP
 250 LET C=0:LET AL=SQR(DS)-RE
 260 PRINT:PRINT "ALTITUDE = ";INT(AL/1000/F1);" ";U$
 270 PRINT "( X = ";INT(XS*SC*2/F2)/2;" ";P$;" )"
 280 PRINT "( Y = ";INT(YS*SC*2/F2)/2;" ";P$;" )"
 290 PRINT "TIME = ";INT(TT/360)/10;" HOURS"
 300 PRINT "C OR S":INPUT A$:RETURN


  10 LET U$="MILES":LET P$="1/10 IN":LET F1=1.609:LET F2=2.54
```

**↖ Line 10 for imperial measurements**

# Spotting satellites

Satellites can be seen at night without any special equipment, although many more can be seen through binoculars. Experienced observers send records of their sightings, including complicated calculations on heights and angles, to scientists, who can work out variations in the Earth's gravitational field from changes in satellite orbits.

## What they look like

Satellites and space stations shine in the night sky when they reflect the Sun, just as the Moon does. Their brightness depends on their size, whether they are coated with shiny material, and how low their orbit is. They look like wandering stars, moving in a different direction from real stars, at about 8km (5 miles) a minute. This is about the same speed as a high-flying aircraft. Large space stations in low orbit are easiest to see, because they reflect sunlight well.

## Looking for a satellite

Look when the night sky is clear. Stand in the darkest part of a garden, making sure that nearby lights are switched off. Watch in the first hour or two after sunset, when it is dark but the Earth's shadow isn't yet high enough to blot out low orbiting satellites. You are more likely to see one if you look in the direction of the Equator.

## Predictions

Satellites are difficult to spot in the sky. But local newspapers often give helpful predictions of those you're likely to see in your local area, up to a distance of 100km (62 miles) from the place specified in the prediction. Astronomical organizations also provide predictions, like the one below. The labels show what each part means.

| Time of appearance | | Direction it rises from. |
|---|---|---|

From Skysville, 18.20 to 18.24 SW 64S SE★

**Direction of highest point it reaches, in degrees.**

**Direction it sinks. An asterix means it will disappear in the Earth's shadow before it goes below the horizon.**

## Photographing satellites

The steps below show you how to photograph a moving satellite. Point your camera in the direction where you know one is due to appear.

**1** Make sure the camera is steady, fixed on a tripod or placed on a firm surface.

**2** Put the camera on a setting of "B", which allows you to keep the shutter open.

**3** When you see the satellite aim the camera, and keep the shutter open for about 5 minutes.

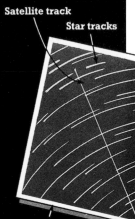

Satellite track

Star tracks

The picture will look like this

## Burn-ups

Satellites burn up brightly when they re-enter the atmosphere. About two satellites a week burn up, but not always at night. It is difficult to predict where or when this will happen.

## Learning more

To learn more about satellite sighting find the address of a local astronomical society from your library, or write to the Astronomical Societies shown below, international organizations which deal with enquiries from all over the world.

The Secretary,
Junior Astronomical Society,
10 Swanwick Walk,
Tadley, Basingstoke,
Hants., England.

The Secretary,
British Astronomical Society,
Burlington House,
Piccadilly,
London,
England.

DANGER: Never look at the Sun through binoculars. You will be blinded for life.

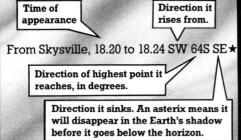

# Space milestones

The list below shows important space missions so far.

**1957** – Sputnik 1 (USSR), first artificial Earth satellite.

**1958** – Explorer 1, first US satellite. Discovered Van Allen belts.

**1960** – Tiros 1 (US), first meteorological satellite. Transit 1B (US), first navigational satellite. Midas 2 (US), first missile early warning satellite.

**1961** – Vostock 1 (USSR), Yuri Gagarin is the first man in space, Telstar 1 (US), first commercial comsat, transmitted live TV between America/Europe.

**1963** – Vostock 6 (USSR), Valentina Tereshkova is the first woman in space.

**1964** – Syncom 3 (US), first comsat in geostationary orbit, transmits from the Tokyo Olympics.

**1965** – Voshkod 2 (USSR), Alexai Leonov performs first spacewalk (10 minutes).

**1966** – Gemini 8 (US), first docking in space.

**1969** – Apollo 11 (US), Neil Armstrong is the first man on the Moon.

**1971** – Launch of Salyut 1 (USSR), first space station.

**1972** – Landsat 1 (US), first Earth resources satellite.

**1973** – Launch of Skylab, first US space station.

**1974** – Launch of Salyut 2 (USSR), which failed in orbit. Launch of Salyut 3, Salyut 4. Russian Soyuz and American Apollo manned spacecraft dock in orbit.

**1976** – Launch of Salyut 5.

**1977** – Launch of Salyut 6.

**1978** – First double docking (USSR), Soyuz 26 and 27 docked with Salyut 6. Progress 1 (USSR), first unmanned supply ferry to space station, first refuelling in space.

**1981** – Columbia (US), first Shuttle spaceflight.

**1982** – Launch of Salyut 7. Two satellites launched from shuttle Columbia.

**1983** – Spacelab (US), first flight on board Shuttle.

**1984** – Shuttle Challenger, first use of MMU. First retrieval, repair and relaunch of satellite.

# Satellite words

**Antenna:** Equipment, either on board a satellite or on the ground, which receives or sends microwave signals.

**Apogee:** The furthest point of a non-circular satellite orbit from Earth.

**DBS:** Short for direct broadcast satellite. These broadcast strong signals carrying TV channels to small ground receiving dishes.

**Docking:** The process of locking two spacecraft securely together in space.

**Footprint:** The reception area on Earth of a satellite microwave signal.

**Geostationary orbit:** An orbit at a height of 35,786 km (22,237 miles), in an easterly direction above the Equator, taking 24 hours for one revolution.

**Gravity:** A pulling force between objects. Its effect keeps spacecraft in orbit.

**Ground station:** Installation on Earth that receives or sends satellite signals.

**Microwaves:** A kind of radio wave used by satellites to send and receive information.

**Orbit:** The path of a satellite around a planet. A thin elliptical path is called an eccentric orbit.

**Orbital velocity:** Speed, dependent on height, which a satellite must maintain to stay in orbit.

**Perigee:** The nearest point of a non-circular satellite orbit to Earth.

**Period:** The time a satellite takes to orbit the Earth once.

**Polar orbit:** An orbit travelling over both Poles of the Earth.

**Radiometer:** A satellite instrument which measures different types of radiation reflected or emitted from objects.

**Rocket:** A launch vehicle powered by fuel burning with an oxidizer, producing exhaust gases.

**Satellite:** An object which orbits a larger object – the Earth in the case of space satellites. A space station is a manned satellite.

**Signature:** The quantity of each wavelength of electromagnetic radiation emitted or reflected by an object.

**Solar cell:** Cell made of silicon which converts the energy of the Sun's rays into electricity.

**Transfer orbit:** A temporary satellite orbit between an initial low orbit and a final high orbit.

# Index

First published in 1985 by Usborne Publishing Ltd, 20 Garrick Street, London WC2E 9BJ, England.

Copyright © 1985 Usborne Publishing Ltd.

The name Usborne and device are Trade Marks of Usborne Publishing Ltd. All rights reserved. No part of this publication may be reproduced, stored in any form or by any means mechanical, electronic, photocopying, recording or otherwise without the prior permission of the publisher.

**48**

Picture credits: Meteosat image – Daily Telegraph Picture Library. Landsat image – National Remote Sensing Centre.
The publishers would like to thank the following for their help: NASA, Hughes Aircraft Company, Novosti, British Aerospace, AEG-Telefunken.

Printed in Spain   D.L.B. 30235-1985